Brassica Park

To Joules,
for patience

BRASSICA PARK

The Final Book in
THE PLANET DWELLER SERIES

THE PLANET DWELLER
MOVING MOOSEVAN
DUCKBILL SOUP

by

Jane Palmer

DODO BOOKS

Other science fiction books by this author

BABEL'S BASEMENT
THE KYBION
THE PLANET DWELLER
MOVING MOOSEVAN
NIGHTINGALE
HUNDER
THE ATON BIRD

Fiction
BALD WENDY
MOSS

CHAPTER 1

Des and Bluebill looked in disbelief at the huge nest of biscuit wrappings and half-empty cartons of convenience meals. The stench was so stiff it felt as though it was trying to push them back out of the ventilation shaft.

Bluebill poked the disgusting heap with her tongs. Several small lizards hissed angrily and scuttled away.

'Can't be reptiles that made it. The vermin needed hands to carry this stuff.'

The colour left Des's scales. 'You mean, BB - we've got an infestation of MAMMALS?'

'Reckon so.'

'None of those critters are large enough to push those trolleys up here from the shopping precinct.'

'Well, it wasn't a lizard. And look,' Bluebill poked something decaying beneath a chewed packet of macaroni cheese. 'Lizards didn't make those teeth marks. That rat was well chewed by something much larger.'

Des fought back the urge to throw up. 'No lizard would dare take on a rat that size anyway.'

'S'right. We're talking monkeys here - bloody large monkeys.'

'Large enough to block the main ventilation shaft with shopping trolleys?'

'With the deposit they demand for those things, it sure as hell wasn't customers. The infestation must have been here for weeks and only comes out at night.'

'Well BB, the only way to be certain is to find their spore.'

Bluebill peered down each shaft that led away from the main ventilation junction. Between them and the small grids of light in the far distance was eerie darkness. She thoughtfully scratched her small ear fin. The monkeys they knew were vicious little critters at the best of times. Des and her were vegetarian and had

1

much slower reflexes. They wouldn't have stood a chance if something was laying in wait with tetanus-infected claws and a jumbo bag of frozen parsnips.

There was a faint shuffling from the vent leading down to the supermarket.

Des unclipped his rod and played out the noose on the end of it as far as it would go. Anything could be waiting in the shadows ahead. Depending on what they encountered, it was a long drop through the escape trapdoor and onto the lids of the freezers below.

Bluebill turned on her helmet's lamp and its beam converged with Des's.

There was scuffling ahead. It could have been a whole nest. Then came rustling from behind them... and in all of the adjoining ventilation shafts.

Des and Bluebill had crawled into an ambush.

Bluebill kicked the bolts securing the trapdoor and it clattered open, allowing piles of detritus to fall onto the freezers below as her camera rapidly flashed away at the large, looming shapes in the darkness of each shaft. As they were briefly illuminated they could tell that these fearsome primates were flesh-eaters and hungry.

Des and Bluebill turned to each other in panic and were momentarily dazzled by their own torches.

That was all the time the vermin needed.

As they pounced, Bluebill seized Des and hauled him through the trapdoor after her.

They landed on top of the freezers and were unconscious for over a day.

The investigation team examined the snaps she had taken.

It wasn't pretty.

CHAPTER 2

'Just what are these creatures, for pity's sake?'

Being a peaceful sort of species, there wasn't much call for soldiers, so the adjutant had to count her fingers to make sure she had the right number before risking a salute.

'No idea, Marm. Intelligence reckons the result of some experiment.'

Her superior scowled. 'Experiment? What scientist on this planet has the facilities to create primates like these?'

'None, Marm. Looks as though they might have escaped from Home World.'

'In a spaceship? They couldn't even open most of the packets they stole from that supermarket.'

'Well, not many of us can either, Marm.'

'These creatures must have been planted here.'

'It does seem the most likely explanation.'

'I always knew that those carnivores would think up something to destabilize this planet one day.'

'They've not succeeded yet. Why should these simians make it any easier?'

'Don't know, but I've got an unpleasant feeling about them. What did you say that scientist reckons they are?'

'Some hominid made up from monkey DNA. He read about the experiments the Dozaurs were doing several years back, and didn't think they would get anywhere.'

'A hominid?'

'Sort of experiment into what monkeys might have evolved into if dinosaurs hadn't made it first. Called them something like "oomans", or was it, "hoomans"?

CHAPTER 3

Higher beings had been eavesdropping on the conversation about "hoomans".

Angry ripples lingered in the rarefied atmosphere for quite some while.

The Supreme Guardian ceased to be nebulous long enough to explode with sufficient rage to make a dent in the quantum reality her kind inhabited.

'I'm sure we can put things to rights-' Reniola tried to bluster, but no longer had a plausible enough body to do it in.

'Every time you attempted to put things right, you made matters worse!'

There was only one way out - blame someone else.

'It's all Diana's fault. If she hadn't insisted we save Moosevan as well as her planet, none of this would have happened.'

'She is a mere mortal!'

'But Moosevan is a cosmic being; she could exist for aeons,' Dax interceded.

'Couldn't either of you work out anything preferable to dragging a moon from Earth's prehistory, making a solar necklace of the system's terrestrial bodies, and turning the humans into dinosaurs?'

'With a bit of luck, Diana may not remember she used to be a human being,' added Dax hopefully.

'Of course she will. The population is living in a delusion. Humans do not have the mental capacity to comprehend that everything is just a quantum possibility. As soon as she persuades others what has happened to them and that they inhabit a moon from their prehistory, all your meddling with her solar system will unravel. And you know what that means.'

Reniola puffed out her molecules to hazard a guess. 'They'll turn back into humans and declare war on their home planet, Earth?'

'One of many plausible, unpleasant possibilities for which you will be responsible.'

Dax had a foreboding about what was expected of her and Reniola. 'You need us to go back there and sort things out?'

'You are the only ones who can comprehend how this confusion was created.' The Supreme Guardian was overestimating their grasp of any reality, quantum or otherwise.

'Are you sure there is no one else?'

'The only other alternative would be to delete the problem.'

Dax and Reniola knew what that meant. The Cosmic Corrector was the universal bleach used to wipe away the tangles in the reality of less evolved mortals. A plasma machine lacking empathy, the only independent action allowed it was to select a suitable mortal to instruct it. That way, no one else needed to take the blame for the consequences.

In her own addled thoughts, Reniola had become fond of Diana and her friends. 'You wouldn't really... Would you?'

'If that is what it takes to restore normality.'

'Someone would have to instruct it?' Dax offered carefully.

'I know. So it won't be either of you two. Now go. Transmit your useless atoms back to the dimension where mortals still know what it is to get a headache.'

CHAPTER 4

Diana and Yuri took it in turns to peer through his ten inch reflector at the distant building site.

'Niet! Niet!' He yanked the telescope down. 'You are too near sun.'

'Sorry, I just saw this large container being driven in. Wonder what's in it?'

'They perhaps make aquarium for flying fish.'

'I bet even Daphne Trotter doesn't know what they're up to, and she was the one to sell them the family cabbage patch.'

'She is only landowner on this planet unscrupulous enough to sell land to planet of carnivores.'

'I'm glad it's over two miles away, even if it is only supposed to be a theme park.'

Yuri absent-mindedly combed his grizzled explosion of hair with his fingers. 'But no one tell us what theme.'

Diana stopped gazing though the eyepiece. 'You know, just lately I've been getting this uneasy feeling.'

For Yuri it was a permanent state of mind, when sober or otherwise. 'I have uneasy feeling for long, long time.'

'You should lay off the cycad juice, it rots the brain.'

If Yuri had a brick for every time he had been told that, he would have been able to build a fifty-foot high wall round his cottage. Yet his tongue didn't feel as though it belonged to his mouth, and why did he have so much hair? Although he felt as though he was entitled to it, most of his species had only managed to grow fine fur to protect the top of the head.

And the planets...? All the stars seemed to be in the right place, but there was something wrong with the planets girdling the sun in the same orbit as the Earth. All the books written by sober astronomers said that was what they were supposed to do, yet it didn't make gravitational or mathematical sense. Deep down, Yuri knew it was absurd that so many terrestrial worlds were in one orbit and the solar system's gas giants had no large moons. There was either something wrong, or Nature had been in the throes of PMT when she got round to their cosmic corner.

'You're thinking again,' Diana told him. 'You know that there's something wrong as well, don't you?'

Yuri was quiet for some time. 'I feel like cup of mint tea.'

Diana took one last look at the mysterious building site and noticed what was being unloaded from the lorries. 'They must be building a supermarket. I've never seen so many shopping trolleys.'

CHAPTER 5

A large, portly dodo peered down through the branches of the tree. A much slender grey bird beside her preened its startlingly white tail feathers.

'Will you just look at that!' squawked the feathered pouffe. 'We'll have to find out what's in those containers.'

Dax stopped preening. 'Probably only wildlife of some sort.'

'Why would the Dozaurs invest so much in a place like this to rear flocks of meat lizards on a planet of vegetarians? And what are they building a huge supermarket in the middle of those cabbage fields for?'

'New concept in "farm fresh" perhaps?'

The birds gazed at each other, beak to beak. Just what were those carnivorous Dozaurs up to? Some vegetarian enterprise they wouldn't have risked on their own planet because of too many teeth in the lobby groups? Knowing them, it had to be pretty ghastly. And why did they need three square kilometres of prime cabbage growing pasture? Apart from the conglomeration of concrete buildings at its centre, there had been little effort at landscaping. Perhaps whatever was going to be kept there liked cabbages, cauliflower and kale.

The two incongruous birds took off and flapped leisurely towards the tall, forbidding gates, where they perched on a huge neon sign declaring that it was the entrance to BRASSICA PARK.

'Something is very wrong here,' announced Reniola as though that were a novelty to her.

7

'Of course there is.'

'"Contain things", they told us. What was that supposed to mean? How can we "contain things" without interfering?'

'Just remember that this is our last chance,' Dax warned Reniola.

The dodo fluffed out her feathers indignantly. 'They wouldn't really disperse us, would they?'

'It's happened to less deserving entities.'

'I don't think I could start all over again from the bottom. All those mucky, mortal incarnations... I didn't remember how tedious they were until encountering Moosevan - It's all her fault, you know!'

'No it wasn't. The ones responsible for causing the problem aeons ago were just like us. Hopefully they are in the process of clambering back up the greasy pole of mortal incarnations.'

'Serves them right. I just don't see why we should have to join them.'

'If we do, at least you'll be able to take your pick of creator gods to blame. That's how most mortals deal with it. So let's make sure we don't blow it this time.'

Reniola knew that it was an accusation and fluffed out her feathers even more until her large beak almost disappeared. 'Well, in that case, I'll just leave you to it.'

'I wish...' muttered Dax.

Reniola's beak clattered shut. Even she was beginning to understand the humdrum ways of a complicated universe. Perhaps this time she might get things right.

CHAPTER 6

Diana stood gazing in the mirror.

No longer bothered about appearance, she was sure the doppelganger looking back didn't belong to her. Whenever she saw Julia, her daughter, she hardly remembered rearing the teenager. It was as if the fairies had stolen the changeling and left her with a child she didn't recognise.

'Good grief', the middle-aged single mother thought to herself. 'I'll be hearing voices next.'

She went into the kitchen to slice carrots. Diana had no idea what to do with them, but carrots were familiar. So were parsnips, potatoes, swede and broccoli. Cycad nuts weren't. She tossed the ones she had left into the bin, telling herself that they rot the brain.

Was that the real reason?

Diana held a carrot in mid peel and gazed out of the window. Birds - most of them - were familiar, so was Edna, who lived a few doors down in the terrace of cottages, especially when she used to swear at some cat or other.

Cat? What were cats? Diana knew what cats were, even though they never existed.

Now Edna was swearing at one of those lizards that occasionally hunted the small rodents in the meadow between the terrace and Yuri's cottage.

Diana dropped the peeler and carrot into the sink.

'Time of life', she told herself, 'I've always been told it was my time of life. If that was the case, why was a dinosaur going through the menopause? Yes, she remembered the menopause. Any female surviving that wasn't likely to forget it.

Then, as the Supreme Guardian had anticipated, the thunderclap of recall convulsed her mind.

Her world was about to be rocked on its axis and the solar system arranged yet again.

Diana wasn't sure how her planet-inhabiting friend, Moosevan, had divided into many smaller Moosevans. Conversation with the resulting planet dwellers wouldn't be the same: so many minds talking at once would bring on a migraine.

But she had to do something. It was obvious that the human species had been transported to the large moon brought back from prehistory by Reniola some

9

months before. If it had been left where it was it would have deflected that asteroid into the Earth and exterminated the dinosaurs. In this new reality, human beings had not evolved. Most creatures were now descended from dinosaurs while mammals were still scrabbling about to inhabit the few niches left. At least Dax and Reniola had the foresight to ensure that the descendants of true carnivorous dinosaurs remained on Earth while her vegetarian kind was transported to the prehistoric moon.

Diana internally raged at the indignity. Even the writers of the soaps her adolescent daughter perpetually watched on TV could have conjured up something more plausible than that.

As Yuri sauntered into the back garden, several mugs, a washing up bowl and large bunch of carrots hurtled out of the window. As Diana hadn't bothered to open it first, he dodged aside to avoid the hail of shattered crockery and glass.

The astronomer continued on all fours and peered into the kitchen, doormat level. 'This argumentative carrot?'

Diana stood, grasping the kitchen sink as though she wanted to wrench it from its plumbing and hurl that as well. 'How about Dax! You do remember her, don't you?'

Yuri experienced a glimmer of recollection and decided to stay on the floor as a precaution.

He shook his head, trying to dislodge the thought. 'Some new detergent?'

'Try Reniola.'

It did not immediately ring a bell. Then something in the recesses of his addled mind tinkled and he recalled why Diana needed to throw things.

He came in and perched on a stool, silently recalling what had happened to him, the human race, Earth and the Solar System in general. 'We have been ...'

'Conned! We've been conned again!' Diana released the sink unit and sank onto the stool facing him.

'This is not good. I need gin.'

'This is catastrophic. You've only got cycad juice and I need you sober.'

'I need me dead drunk for next six months.'

'I'll phone Salisbury,' she threatened,

That helped steel his resolve. 'He is buffoon and would not know whether he was dinosaur, duck or drag artist.'

'He might have guessed what has happened as well.'

'He has not imagination to guess. He is stuck-up English teacher with pension to think about.'

Diana sighed. 'We have to tell someone, Yuri.'

'And who believe us? We get slot on LOONY STORIES OF THE WEEK perhaps, and one inch in local tabloid underneath ads for rubber underwear.'

'There are plenty of familiar things people might remember.'

'What do you remember?'

'A cat.'

'You never had cat?'

'As in Reniola, and Edna screaming at her.'

Yuri paused. 'So, we get people to believe us. Then what we do?'

Diana hadn't reached that step yet. She could already feel it crumbling and sensed that Yuri was retreating into his own private bubble of defeatism, but she was made of sterner stuff.

CHAPTER 7

Kulp was green, flat-headed, splay-toed and grievously put upon by an unsympathetic Universe. He was also a greedy, unscrupulous, engineering genius. He had been converted from total wickedness by a galactic force for good, only to revert back again - several times - and had still not decided what to do for a pension. The only thing he was sure about was that he would never again get involved with those infernal entities, Dax and Reniola, or human beings of any description. In fact, he would have been elated if someone told him the latter species didn't really exist after all, and his experience of them was all down to the paranoia of genius.

Deluded or not, Kulp had a formidable reputation to live up to. With the rise of the new entrepreneurs who thrived by paddling in the mire which was all that remained of the once mighty Mott empire there was a lot more competition. The Mott had been ghastly, ruthless and mindless, and couldn't have survived without the androids that eventually turned on them. Kulp had found the species easy to outwit, but now wealth flowed through more torturous avenues. Opportunism and amorality was the name of the game. Nothing was straightforward any more and it was becoming harder for old-fashioned criminals of even his mettle to make a living.

CHAPTER 8

An impatient rumpus and raised voices came from inside the container. An access tunnel had been connected to its rear door so it was linked directly to the lobby of the supermarket. The excitement reached a crescendo as the container door was raised.

Its occupants hurtled out to seize the shopping trolleys stacked in regimented rows. There was a blur of bright, baggy shorts, polyester frocks and excruciatingly tight leggings. Small pieces of plastic clutched by each overweight specimen glinted in the hard light.

One of the attendants recoiled. 'What a ghastly sight. Glad I won't be sitting at those checkouts. By the time they've been up and down those aisles several times, they'll be in a right lather.'

'There's omnivores for you,' agreed his partner. 'We'll all live to rue the day these creatures were brought here, mark my words.'

The shopping frenzy carried on until dusk, when the specimens were herded into secure transport which took them to their sleeping quarters where they could hoard their spoils, watch game shows and chat on their smartphones.

Reniola was settling down to roost for the night. 'Do they really intend to let the public into this place?'

'The Dozaurs think that accelerating the evolution of humans by using primate DNA will undermine the vegetarian planet. They want to persuade everyone here that being omnivorous is okay,' Dax explained. 'Once they believe that, eating meat will become acceptable. It's the first step in allowing them to prey on their juicy neighbours once more.'

'You mean there would be enough individuals here to farm their own kind for Dozaur consumption?'

'You've never really delved much into human history, have you?'

'We should never have allowed the Dozaurs to discover space travel. How did they manage that as well as genetic engineering, given how few of them developed enough intellect for basic arithmetic?'

'It only takes a few bright sparks in the midden of stupidity. It won't work, of course.'

'And if it does?'

'Things could become even more complicated.'

It had to be stopped of course, before the Cosmic Corrector was sent in to "cleanse" the solar system.

Dax turned and nearly knocked Reniola from the branch with her long tail. 'I've got an idea.'

Reniola felt cheated; that was usually her line. 'What?'

'How many humans do you think the Dozaurs have created?'

'Not that many.' Then a terrible prospect loomed before the dodo. 'Oh no! We can't eradicate them. Only the Cosmic Corrector can, and then only as a last resort.'

'Maybe not, but we can do a little tinkering.'

'How?'

'What if the visitors to Brassica Park don't see humans, but something totally different.'

'So what are you going to put in their place, three-legged vegetables?'

'No, not even organic ones, just something alien.'

'How alien?'

CHAPTER 9

'Come on Yuri, let me in. I know you're there.'

It wasn't unusual for Yuri to bolt his cottage door when he saw Dr Eva Hopkirk coming. She may have been his wife, and paid for his cottage, reflector and dietary needs, including the gut-rot cycad juice, but she was also another astronomer. They would have probably got on reasonably well if she hadn't been in charge of an observatory with several radio telescope dishes and a one and a half metre reflector, when all he had was a ten inch reflector in his front garden.

The resentment was often palpable.

'I've got something you have to see,' Eva persisted.

14

She might have only wanted to show him an Argos catalogue, or demands for the last two years community charge, but the door remained bolted. Yuri remained lying on his back under the table with a bottle and half pint glass.

'You'll like it. These observations are just up your street. Fiona won't give you the chance to see them again if you don't open up now.'

Fiona, Eva's young assistant, resembled a hare standing on its hind legs, even though everyone was supposed to be descended from hadrosaurs. She was usually happy to show Yuri anything he asked for, so why hadn't she brought this amazing material?

Eva must have got hold of something special.

Yuri sat bolt upright and hit his head on the table. Stunned, he crawled to the door on all fours and pulled back its bolt. Eva charged in, tripped over him and collided with the table. Papers from a document folder flew everywhere.

Before she had chance to swear at him, Yuri had snatched up sheets and was examining them. 'These are other planets in same orbit.'

'Except those on the other side of the sun, of course.' Then Eva realised how badly bruised her hip was. 'You're bloody drunk again, aren't you.'

'No, I was just under table.'

'What the hell for?'

'I like being under table.'

Eva knew better than to argue.

Yuri pointed to the graphs at the bottom of each page. 'What are these figures?'

'The degree each planet had moved in its orbit over the last two weeks. The red circles are mine.'

'I recognise them. No one else make red circles as though with pen of Inquisition.'

'Inquisition', thought Eva. The analogy sounded distantly familiar, though infuriatingly out of reach.

Yuri examined the other papers. The more he put them in order, the more he had difficulty believing his eyes. 'This is not possible.'

'Why d'you think Fiona told me to bring them to you?'

'Why not Fiona bring them?'

'She's trying for promotion. Got some bee in her bonnet about this sort of discovery not looking too good on her CV.'

Yuri sat back on his haunches and clutched the file to him as though the laws of thermodynamics, general relativity and quantum mechanics would all be undermined by it contents.

'Okay, now what's the matter?'

'You not believe me.'

'Look, I don't want to believe Fiona's figures, but that girl doesn't make mistakes. So anything you tell me can't be much worse than more than a dozen planets jiggling about in the same orbit.'

Yuri shook his grizzled locks. 'Oh, but you are wrong, Dr Hopkirk.'

Eva went to the table and poured herself a generous measure of Yuri's gut rot. 'All right, let me have a shot of this first.'

'Gin would be much better.'

'Gin? What's Gin?'

'Ah, it was not such a great friend of yours. I remember it well, though.'

'Gin? You're not going flaky again, are you?'

'Many times I wish this was so.'

'Come on. If you know something about these planets' erratic behaviour, you'd better own up. There's no astronomical reason for it.'

'Why not other observatories see same thing?'

'Probably have. Just don't want to be first to publish.'

Yuri remained quiet, watching Eva in his owl-like manner until she had drained her glass, before announcing, 'They are not really planets, you know.'

She choked on the last dregs of fermented cycad juice. 'What?'

'Except Mars and Venus - they could not convert Mercury, it was too carbonized, one side frozen solid, other like furnace. It might have cracked laterally if moved to Goldilocks zone.'

'Mars and Venus?' scoffed Eva. 'What on Earth are-' She stopped as a peel of bells from recognition's belfry rang out. 'Earth,' she said, and then went so quiet, Yuri thought his wife had gone into shock until she announced, 'We're not on Earth, are we?'

'As we are Earthlings, would you not say this was odd?'

Dr Eva Hopkirk was angry, bewildered and looking over that precipice at the edge of sanity her husband was so familiar with. 'What in God's name made me bring that folder here?'

'Because you are not happy, but great astronomer would never admit to herself there are many things her puny science cannot explain.'

'Okay Einstein, you explain it.'

'Not without Diana.'

'I should have known. Why don't you propose to her so I can get a divorce?'

'She cannot afford to keep me.'

'For someone with her head screwed on against the thread, she knows when she's well off.' Eva rose unsteadily. 'All right, let's go and see your girlfriend.'

CHAPTER 10

Kulp swore softly as he added the finishing touches to his latest venture. Oh that the brilliance of a mind like his should be lowered to construct such things. He was capable of installing gravity tunnels to hop - or in his case, clatter painfully along because he never bothered with such feeble extras as stabilizers - to another galaxy. Unfortunately, the only other galaxy available to him had been the Milky Way, and the only planet he could reach with any certainty had been the Earth.

Given that the species which had recently acquired it were the direct descendants of carnivorous dinosaurs, he should have known it would not be the ideal place for retirement. But the gravitational blip that was pinning the galaxies together across millions of light years was beginning to weaken. Kulp's galaxy was on the verge of being sucked into oblivion, and it would no longer be possible to reach anywhere. The Universe had put up with this rotten apple for long enough and was in the process of evicting the galaxy from the cosmic barrel. Not even Kulp could guess where it would end up; he was just relieved he wouldn't be around to see it.

Though Kulp hated to admit it, Jannu, his old assistant in crime, would have been able to equip the massive tourist ark he had constructed using robot workers much faster. Even Tolt, an ex waste disposal engineer, however inept at everything else, could have efficiently judged the stress on the hull as it approached the odd pulsar or white dwarf.

Now there was a market driven economy. Gone were the days you could inexpensively ship out waste so toxic it risked falling through the crust of the planet receiving it, or just push it into the nearest black hole, even jettison the odd batch of refugees fleeing from the Mott hoards to take on more cargo. Now, if you couldn't afford the insurance, you risked being sued for losing someone's nearest and dearest down a disposal vent, or exposing them to fatal drops in pressure because the triple glazing in the viewing dome was too thin.

However much he tried not to think about it, Kulp knew he was lucky to be alive. If he was ever caught and returned to his Olmuke home planet, that arrangement would not last for long. The population had still not found a way of removing the pink dye he sprayed on them during his freelance outlaw days. Having escaped from them once, it wasn't likely they would bother forging another cage for him.

Kulp called in the last robot. The hull was now pressurized enough to deflect the collision with a neutron star, and the cabins were immaculate, right down to the last acid proof tableware for silicon life forms. Although the venture was demeaning for an engineer of his mettle, with a fleet of these arks crewed by robots he could as last make that fortune to retire on. He had mapped out routes to some of the most spectacular star systems in the unstable galaxy using gravitational anomalies so the cruise wouldn't take anyone's lifetime.

Now for the ultimate indignity: something no android, however well-programmed or personable, could do.

The first unsuspecting tourists were impressed at how much their golden Salac female guide knew about engineering. The green Kulp was oddly convincing in that disguise. How could they have known she was a galactic criminal trying to make an honest living? And who wanted to see a toad-like Olmuke inviting you on board a vessel about to visit some of the most dangerous corners of the galaxy?

On the down payments alone, Kulp would be able to construct another ark, so it looked as though Googa, the Salac female, was here to stay.

CHAPTER 11

'Oh Mum... Mavis says it's quite safe. They've got armed guards at every entrance.'

Diana tried to sound firm. 'Look Julia, I am not paying that amount of money just to see some mindless anthropoids pushing trolleys round a supermarket.'

'But she says they're ever so funny, with their little pieces of plastic. They use them to buy everything, whether they want it or not, and knock over stacks of things to be first at the special offers, and fight at the checkouts...'

There is a point when the whine of an adolescent voice can either trigger tinnitus or break down the resolve of the most fearsome doorkeeper. At that moment, Diana didn't want to swallow yet another painkiller and agreed to take her.

Had the queue realised that the Brassica Park had been thought up by their arch enemies, the Dozaurs whose only regard for them was as food, it probably wouldn't have been so long. Little did they know that they were confirming their carnivorous cousins' belief about herbivores flocking for no sensible reason.

The visitors passed through the turnstiles and into the carriages of an overhead train. Below, a Gordian knot of roads was being laid through the acres of cabbage to provide an even more ambitious display of the anthropoids, though it would be some while before enough specimens were reared to provide entertaining traffic jams.

The carriages slowly moved off, passing over some adolescent "hoomans" tapping away furiously at small, brightly lit tablets, oblivious of the drop of several feet into the foundations being laid for housing. One of the preoccupied teenagers managed to walk straight into it. An attendant, obviously familiar with the problem, rapidly pulled the screeching girl out by the loop on the end of the pole. He daren't think what would happen when the street was finished and the adult exhibits had access to the pub at its far end. At least it would mean overtime.

He shrugged off the foulmouthed abuse the young woman hurled at him and went back to his soundproof booth to watch the security monitors, and a game show which the Dozaurs were losing. It was just as well they lived on another planet; they were summing up the triumphant vegetarian opponents as a potential meal.

Diana shuddered at the spectacle below. The timpani of bells ringing in her memory were now being played by the demented campanologists from reality's nightmare. It was obvious that no one else in the carriage were having their memories jogged at the sight of the texting teenagers. Diana longed for someone to leap free of their seat belt and proclaim that they were victims of an alien illusion. On second thoughts, although it might have saved her sanity, they would have all risked being put away for public safety.

Julia was lapping everything up, from the socially inept adolescents to the machinery building the high concrete blocks in which the first residents were already being housed. It was evident a few had been there some while because small lizards scavenged amongst the refuse sacks and fought over the occasional bone. No one in the carriage had ever seen anything like it, except Diana.

They didn't know how lucky they were.

'What's the matter, mum? You've gone a funny colour?'

'Just wait until we get inside that supermarket, then I'll go the same shade as an Olmuke.'

'What's an Olmuke, Mum?'

Diana had no idea what made her say that. 'If you can't remember Kulp, you're capable of forgetting your own name.'

Julia didn't bother to wonder what her mother was on about, it only wasted good ogling time, and they were coming up to the main attraction... the supermarket.

CHAPTER 12

From the safety of his ground control Kulp, disguised as Googa the Salac female, waved to the passengers on the ark as it slowly ascended through the thin atmosphere. When it was fifty miles above the planet, he switched control over to the robot pilot. Nothing could go wrong. There were two thousand souls with litigious relatives on board, and he couldn't afford it to. When some species sued, it was usually for body parts of the defendant: others with a judgement in their favour just dissolved the offender with an accurately aimed sneeze of sulphuric acid.

As the vessel disappeared from his tracking system, Kulp relaxed. Even Jannu and Tolt would have been impressed at seeing the gleaming star cruiser depart... and they hated him.

Kulp had hardly started to tally up how much that tour would bring in when his control room disappeared.

He was standing in a brightly lit corridor of shelves.

There was the burbling of annoying music, and he was grasping a supermarket trolley.

CHAPTER 13

'Trust Diana to be out when we need her!' cursed Eva after hammering her back door like a Fury. She turned on Yuri. 'Now you'll have to tell me without her help.'

Yuri was cornered. There were no tin hats to protect him from Dr Hopkirk and it was a long dash back across the meadow to his cottage on his short legs. Nothing could save him this time. He would have to own up and once again run the risk of being committed. Marrying her in the first place must have been proof enough he was certifiable, even if the only other option at the time was returning to a place where a man wearing pink risked being beaten up.

Yuri was about to surrender to fate when salvation came from the most unlikely source. This was indeed a quantum universe filled with the strangest uncertainties.

Striding through the side passage was his arch rival, a tall English don named Salisbury.

Eva was momentarily put off guard at the arrival the distinguished figure.

'I say,' he said. 'Is something wrong? I can't make anyone in at the front.'

Yuri suddenly realised how insanely jealous he was of the man. 'Diana? What you want with Diana?' he snarled.

'Just wanted to tell her about this odd...' Salisbury remembered how prickly Yuri could be and thought better of going on.

'This odd what?' demanded Eva.

The small woman in the white overalls had a gaze penetrating enough to staple closure notices on the doors of vice dens. She was the stern flip side of the excitable Yuri.

Salisbury wasn't inclined to engage her in a battle of willpower. 'Just this and that.'

There were very few rare occasions when Yuri closed ranks with his wife. 'What is this, and what is that?'

Against the judgement of his commonsense fairy, the scholar started to explain, 'Well, I woke up a couple of mornings ago and started marking some papers on creative writing. You know the sort of thing.' It was obvious by her expression that Eva still had trouble believing the Big Bang wasn't a cosmic practical joke and already radiated scepticism, so he didn't try to elucidate. 'One of the students came up with this review of a book that had not been written.'

'Well, certainly sounds creative to me.'

'Goodness knows where she got the idea. It was about a park of dinosaurs.'

'Dinosaurs?' mouthed Yuri.

'Dozaurs?' said Eva.

Inexplicably, the scholar was momentarily lost for words, and then rallied. 'I asked Jacqueline about it afterwards. She had no idea what she had been thinking and believed it must have been from a vivid dream she confused with reality. When I spoke to Diana over the phone, she said that a similar park was being built near here, and then - I remembered...' Salisbury froze in mid sentence at the terror of it. For a moment it looked as though he might topple over like a felled skittle, and only just managed to regain his balance as he realised neither of the other two were going to catch him. 'I remembered everything!'

Salisbury was so unsettled at admitting the self-revelation he would have dashed away if Eva hadn't caught his jacket.

'We all need to talk.'

Now wishing he had said nothing, Salisbury was marched up the meadow to Yuri's cottage.

CHAPTER 14

Julia had her nose flattened against the carriage window, wondering at the exhibits waddling up the aisles of the shopping mall. 'Aren't they huge, Mum. What do they eat to get to that size?'

'Other animals mainly.'

There was the groan of disgust from the other passengers as well as Julia.

Diana couldn't contain herself any longer. 'You don't get it, do you? Those freezers directly below us are filled with the flesh of other creatures! Just wait until you all snap out of this fantasy and start craving a bacon sandwich!'

'Mum...'

The horrified expressions had no effect on Diana. 'Then you can return to that fantasy where the flesh of other animals is just magicked onto the supermarket shelves as though the wretched creatures were only too happy to donate their body parts.'

'Mum!'

'What!'

'They've all suddenly disappeared.'

For one chilling moment Diana thought the other passengers had been tossing themselves from the carriage to escape her outburst.

Julia sounded indignant. 'All the shoppers and their trolleys just scuttled away. Something down there scared them off. Why do you think they're hiding?'

'Probably run out of credit. There are only so many packets of crisps, cans of cola and beefburgers you can buy with a float of two thousand pounds a day.'

'Do they really eat and drink all that stuff, Mum? It can't be any good for them.'

Diana gave up. It was obvious no one had taken in a word she had said. 'That's what makes them "hoomans". If they had a healthy diet they'd probably turn into a different species.'

'Mum! Mum! I think you're right. Look!' Julia pointed excitedly to a figure standing stock still in stunned surprise between the shelves of baked beans and spaghetti hoops.

Everyone in the carriage craned over to take a look. It tilted so dangerously on the overhead rail the emergency brake cut in and they ground to a halt.

'Mum! Mum! What is it?'

Mum wasn't sure right away.

Then the head jerked up and the strange creature appeared to recognise her. Its wide mouth opened in amazement. The huge golden wig of spikes and curls slowly slid from its flat, green pate and golden makeup dribbled from its face under the supermarket's hot lights.

'Ugh, how ghastly,' Julia complained.

The hubbub about them suggested that the other passengers were just as repelled.

Diana stared back in disbelief, not daring to twitch a muscle in case someone realised she and Kulp knew each other. That would have been far worse than her rant about meat eaters.

But now there was something more interesting.

'And there are two more!' went up the cry.

'Look, look, just by the lemonade! But they're green as well. Nothing in the brochure said anything about them being green.'

'Good grief,' Diana muttered to herself. 'Jannu and Tolt. This can only mean one thing.'

Dax and Reniola were back.

'Mum, Mum, you're talking to yourself.'

'You really want me to start ranting again?'

'What are they doing here, Mum? These aren't really the "hoomans", are they?'

Diana recovered enough composure to lapse back into parent mode. 'How would I know? No one apart from your friend Mavis and a school party have ever seen them before now.'

'They didn't say anything about them being green, and that ugly. And they're not very lively, are they?'

The rest of the visitors remained intrigued by the spectacle. There may have only been three of the specimens, but they were certainly different from what was expected. These were a world away from the portly, pink-kneed specimens with too much hair and penchant for cream cakes and animal flesh.

These exhibits were rather splendid in their ghastly green way. They had to be genetically engineered - there was no way a sane Mother Nature could have thought them up.

The safety brakes at last allowed the carriage to move, leaving Kulp and his companions, standing, stock still with horror, at their predicament.

CHAPTER 15

'This is not happening... This is not happening...' Diana was repeating over and over again under her breath.

Julia was too busy buying postcards from the souvenir shop to notice. The mother she had once remembered as being cool, calm and collected, had turned into an unpredictable enigma as soon as she had hit the menopause. She could suddenly appear out of nowhere as though she had been to another planet and back, and talk to the furniture - or was it that voice in her head again? Ranting on about the oddest things when in public was the worst. Juliet never knew where to look, and had frequently pretended they weren't together. Despite it all, the teenager still had to admit that living with Diana was far more interesting than the lives her friends had in their humdrum families.

Julia looked up from the shelves groaning with the effigies of the tubby humans. Now where had her mother gone? She had better check to make sure she wasn't in trouble. It was a pity Yuri wasn't with them. He was totally disorganised and irrational, which seemed to cancel out her mother's foibles to make up one relatively sane couple. (Or so Julia thought, but she didn't know the half of it. She was going to be mortified when the truth dawned or - being a teenager - perhaps not.)

She found Diana outside the gates of Brassica Park, looking about as though Dozaurs had prepared an ambush.

'What's up Mum?'

Diana snapped back to her daughter's reality. 'Nothing, nothing at all.'

'You were looking for something, weren't you?'

'Of course not.' It was obviously a lie. 'You can get home by yourself can't you?'

"Course I can.'

Diana gave Julia her bus fare and told her to stay with Yuri until she returned. Then she went back to scouring the hedgerows for a large angular cat. But no, surely not even Reniola would be confused enough to opt for that disguise again on a planet where there weren't any moggies. So what would she become this time? Hopefully it would not be wearing an ankle-length frock made from Laura Ashley curtains.

Even if it meant walking the perimeter of the huge Brassica Park, Reniola wasn't going to get away with it this time. Intergalactic superbeing or not, she had gone too far. Whatever Reniola decided to disguise herself as, it would be impossible to mistake.

And there she was... Not many dodos sat in trees grinning beakily at everything going on below them.

Most of the visitors had dispersed, jabbering amongst themselves at the spectacle of Kulp, Tolt and Jannu clutching supermarket trolleys, in shock at no longer being in the galaxy of their choice.

Diana glowered at the feathered anomaly. 'Not funny Reniola!'

The bird tried to ignore her, but Reniola didn't know how to be aloof for very long. 'Don't worry old thing, it was only Kulp and his friends.' Then something occurred to the entity. 'Ah, you've worked it all out, haven't you?'

'Just how obtuse did you think we were.'

'Well, we couldn't be sure at first-'

'That wasn't a question!'

The bird peered down apologetically. 'Sorry. Can't say too much though. We're on a secret mission.'

'Secret mission?'

'Well, just keeping things under wraps until...'

'What things?'

'I'd rather you didn't ask.'

'I'm asking.'

'Well, there is this entity called the Cosmic Corrector ...' Then Reniola realised that she shouldn't have said even that and her beak clattered shut.

Diana was tempted to hurl her handbag in the hope of knocking Reniola out of the tree, then thought better of it. 'What's Dax up to?'

'Dax?'

'Yes, you remember Dax. As incompetent as you, but with more style.'

'Oh, she's just fluttered off somewhere. Needs to have a word with Kulp.'

'I'm glad I can't understand a word that Olmuke says. I shouldn't think they're going to be very pleasant ones.' Diana realised she was being sidetracked. 'So just what is this Cosmic Corrector then? I suppose it does what it says on the label?'

'It needs to be fine-tuned first. It's a sort of... machine,' Reniola admitted reluctantly.

Diana didn't have a clue what the entity was on about. Then an idea crossed her mind. Dax and Reniola had always been free agents, but now appeared to be on their best behaviour... which shouldn't have been sur-prising after rearranging the solar system. So that meant they were now answerable to a higher authority. And that authority would be the ones who dispatched this Cosmic Corrector. The more Diana thought about it, the more convinced she became that it did actually do what it said on the label.

'Okay then,' Diana said. 'See you about.'

Anyone else would have been suspicious about the change in tone.

Reniola sat pondering for a few moments after Diana had left, and then flapped her absurd, ungainly wings. She had discovered that it was best to get them going before leaving her perch. Eventually she blundered into the air.

Diana flagged down the automatic taxi she had summoned on her phone and ordered its computer, 'Follow that bird.'

CHAPTER 16

Salisbury peered distastefully at the dregs of tea in his enamel mug and wished he hadn't drunk it. 'Well how could it have been anything to do with me?' he protested. 'I never had any affinity with those stupid entities. I always assumed that they were your friends.'

The mere thought triggered a stream of expletives in Russian from Yuri as he raised his fists at the opponent over a foot taller than he was.

'Just a minute, just a minute,' intervened Eva before her husband and the English don came to blows. 'Let's get this straight. We, the human race, are marooned on one of the Earth's prehistoric moons, which should have been destroyed sixty million years ago. As a consequence of Dax and Reniola moving it when they did, the dinosaurs survived and went on to evolve into the dominant species?' Yuri nodded. 'But they couldn't get rid of us, so we had to become dinosaurs as well?'

'Only in illusion of course,' corrected Salisbury who had to ensure all the i's were dotted and t's crossed.

Eva went on. 'So this is an illusion that could slip at any moment if enough people start to remember what happened. Then what?'

'I suppose we stop being vegetarians.'

'This I do not want to think about.' Yuri poured another shot of cycad juice into his cold tea and noisily slurped it down.

'Given what humans were like before having respect for all living things imposed on us, it's bound to result in an arms race with the Dozaurs,' Eva deduced.

'And Dozaurs are descendants of tyrannosaurus and allosaurus,' added Yuri.

'I shouldn't think so, old man, they probably evolved from something much smaller and-' Salisbury hesitated.

'Fast enough to devour all herbivores so they now need to farm them.'

Eva folded her arms and gazed out of the window at Julia who was bounding up the meadow towards the cottage, 'So what happens when the illusion does fall apart?'

Salisbury blanched at the thought. 'God knows.'

'Well, if Yuri can sense something is wrong, then whatever is holding everything together must be very tenuous.'

'And I know Diana speaks truth. She will know what to do,' insisted Yuri.

The idea brought out Salisbury's protective streak, 'And what do you expect Diana to do about it?'

'Why not Diana?' stormed Yuri. 'She always makes things right!' He scowled and continued to slurp into his mug.

This was about as much Eva could absorb in one go and she decided to leave the men to argue themselves out.

Just as she opened the door, Julia bounded in.

'Hi Yuri, hi Dr Hopkirk, hi Mr Salisbury. Not interrupting anything, am I? Only Mum says I have to stop with Yuri until she gets back.'

31

'Gets back from where?' asked Eva.

'Not sure, but as the bus pulled away I saw her talking to this funny looking bird.'

CHAPTER 17

Kulp wasn't surprised when the tall, furry creature sauntered casually down the shopping aisle towards him. Unlike Reniola, Dax had discarded her bird persona for the mortal form she had first chosen. Its original owner was now a comfortable universe away and not the litigious sort when it came to personal appearance. The ears were strikingly large and upright, the tail almost as long as her body, and the orange eyes blazed like the headlights of oncoming fate.

Under his ridiculous disguise as a Salac female, Kulp fumed with a rage that defrosted a nearby freezer and was picked up by the smoke alarm directly above him. The Olmuke knew that nothing could damage the entity sauntering towards him - he had tried on numerous occasions - yet he had never felt more like making another attempt.

'Sorry about this Kulp. You were just the first alien that came into my head.'

The idea of going into Dax's head with a hatchet appealed to the Olmuke and he growled with a guttural sound only his species' vocal cords could produce.

'Didn't realise you'd be ...' Dax waved a long hand to indicate his unconventional frock, 'so occupied.'

Kulp was the last person in any galaxy she would have expected to go in for cross-dressing. 'Didn't break up some party, did I?'

Kulp continued to glower.

'We'll send you back to whatever nefarious little scheme you were engaged in as soon as possible of course. But we couldn't have all those humans running about by themselves. Without you and your friends to confuse the issue, people here would have started to realise who they really are. Just pretend you belong here and the guards won't suspect a thing. They don't know how varied these "hoomans" are supposed to be.'

Kulp could only wonder what she had done to persuade them that he was a plausible substitute for a human being. Not even the mortals around here could be that thick - or could they?

The fire alarm went off.

The engineer's brain at last came out of shock mode.

'Where the hell is this?' he demanded.

'Long story. No time.'

'I saw the human female called Diana - only she wasn't looking that human at the time.'

Dax stopped dead in her tracks as though the supermarket's smoke shutter had dropped on her toes. 'Diana?'

'She was in that-' Kulp pointed to the overhead railway.

'Did she recognise you?'

'What, in this get up?' lied Kulp as the sprinkler system saturated his frock.

'Good.' Dax shook the water from her fur and started to fade from sight.

'Just a minute! You can't do this!'

But the elegant alien had gone, leaving Kulp clutching a shopping trolley, huge golden wig, and to explain why the fire alarm had gone off.

At least no one he knew was about to see him in the absurd disguise.

'Well hello Kulp,' a familiar voice sang out derisively above the sound of the alarm. It came from behind the frozen yoghurts.

Kulp couldn't believe his eyes. Not even Dax was evil enough to do this to him. Tolt and Jannu, for ages

33

the struts that supported his sense of self-importance, stood gurgling with delight at his embarrassment.

Kulp knew from experience that these two could be damaged.

Without warning, a well aimed hail of baked bean tins flew in their direction. Some missed; most found their mark.

Not as quick as Kulp, Tolt and Jannu skidded through the puddles towards the sauces and salad dressings. Soon the air was filled with bottles of vinegar, tins of spaghetti hoops and corned reptile meat.

By the time the guards had pumped the supermarket full of tranquillizing gas, the main attraction of the Dozaurs' new theme park was knee deep in water and damaged goods. Tissues, toilet rolls, and sanitary goods bobbed in the scum that had once been the "hooman" delicacies of mayonnaise, barbecue sauce and mashed potato.

After being brainwashed by Dax, the guards had no problem in believing the three Olmuke were just rebellious "hoomans". The manager was more concerned that the experiment had become unstable on his watch and the "hoomans" in his charge had developed a sudden aversion to shopping. They had to be isolated before the idea contaminated the others.

A battalion of cleaners was sent in to deal with the mess so the shelves could be restocked ready for the next visitors. And it had to be done quickly before the Dozaur management found out.

CHAPTER 18

Most automatic taxis worked to a pre-programmed routes and Reniola's leisurely flight path overheated the computer of Diana's as it followed the incongruous bird. But the vehicle was programmed to accept that the customer is always right - unless they caused an accident - and the traffic out there was pretty sparse.

The small taxi darted backwards and forwards across its predetermined grid to keep the aerodynamic absurdity in its sights. Fortunately its engine didn't explode. Customers were inclined to panic and leave without paying if they smelt burning, and this one had a glint of resolve in her eye that suggested she wouldn't have been too bothered if it had burst into flames.

Eventually the ungainly bird lowered its undercarriage and came down in a copse of trees near the museum where Diana had gone back to working part time. On one side towered the radio telescope array of Eva's observatory, and on the other, acres of reconstructed historical buildings.

Diana felt uncomfortable.

Although it was unnervingly close to home, this land belonged to the Trotter family who had used it for blood sports. Most animals with sense had moved out long ago, but it was the last rural bastion they could lay claim to. They had been obliged to sell all their other land to farmers and Dozaur property developers who didn't take no for an answer, even from that influential clan of landed gentry.

Diana off paid the taxi at the museum gates. As soon as the card had been validated it shot back to its rank with a high-pitched whine of relief.

However much she wanted to investigate the copse of trees where the dodo had landed, it would have meant leaving Julia and Yuri to their own devices for too long. Her adolescence and his addled grasp of reality meant, given time, some mischief would result. And at that moment Diana did not have the time to deal with it.

When she arrived at his cottage her fears were confirmed.

Eva, Yuri, Salisbury, and Julia had convinced themselves that the end of the world was nigh and that Diana was the only person who could do anything about it.

Yuri drunkenly sighed from under his table. 'It is pity we have no Moosevan to contact any more.'

Salisbury didn't comment. The planet dweller who had briefly inhabited the Earth after her world had been destroyed was impossible to imagine, even before she split into umpteen different planet dwellers. At least that must have considerably reduced the fascination she had with both of the men.

When Diana arrived Eva at last decided to apply logic to the situation. 'As the other worlds in our orbit are showing signs of eccentric motion, it must be caused by the new planet dwellers inhabiting them.' The astronomer assumed her friend didn't need briefing on the problem as she no doubt had a hand in creating it in the first place.

Everyone looked at Diana.

Diana looked at Yuri.

He sobered up at the implication and rolled from under the table. 'Oh no, I have done with passionate planets. They are not good for sanity-'

As though to confirm Yuri's worst fears, the illusion they had been held fast in momentarily weakened and they briefly saw each other as they really were. The chink in reality closed before Yuri could seize the bottle of cycad juice and find out whether he was really drinking gin.

Eva was just as disconcerted. 'That wasn't good.'

'Why not?' asked Julia. 'Why shouldn't everything go back to the way it was?'

'We're not on Earth. The human race doesn't realise that this isn't its planet. It will go out of its mind with panic. You remember panic, don't you Diana? And you know what people do when they panic. Not all of them go shopping!'

Diana was cornered. 'All right! All right! I've just got the feeling something else even more serious is about to happen.'

'More serious!?' echoed Salisbury.

'Even Reniola sounded worried about it. And you know how dense she is.'

'So what do we do?'

There was no answer to that, so Diana suggested, 'I think it would be a good idea if we all slept on it.'

'I think that is right,' agreed Yuri. 'Only problem is, we have to wake up.'

'What're you up to?' Eva asked Diana.

'Look, first you expect me to do something, then become suspicious when you think I might. You can't have it both ways, Eva.'

Eva had always insisted on having everything both ways. It was her way of dealing with tedious reality. Like light particles, her reasoning could travel either in packets or waves. She may have been a slave to logic, but did not necessarily think in straight lines. Quantum uncertainty ruled and it was probably best to stay where they were until one of the stupid entities who created the cosmic shipwreck in the first place decided to do something about it. The problem with that was, everyone could drown before they threw them lifebelts.

Julia yawned. Being in her early teens, these life and death matters seemed more like the pilot for a new TV series without the guns and explosions - they would probably come later. 'Mum, was those green things we saw at the theme park Olmukes?'

'Were those green things,' Salisbury automatically corrected her, before his empty enamel mug clattered to the floor. 'Olmukes!!'

'Ah,' Diana guiltily evaded. 'Didn't say anything because I didn't want to alarm you.'

Julia wasn't yet mature enough to know when to keep quiet. 'One of them looked really strange. It was wearing a huge wig... with curls.'

'A wig. An Olmuke wearing a wig?' Salisbury

gasped in horror.

'Kulp actually,' Diana reluctantly admitted as she slapped the back of her daughter's head and sent the diamante slide fastening her hair spinning across the room.

'Mum,' she wailed, 'that was my best slide.'

At the mention of the one creature in the universe they could mutually loathe, Salisbury and Yuri looked ready to run a two minute mile.

'Don't worry about it,' Diana reassured them, 'He and his friends are safely locked away.'

'They may be safe, but are we?' demanded Salisbury.

'How you not mention this to me?' scolded Yuri. 'Now I not sleep at all.'

'I told you, they're nothing to worry about.'

'How they get here?'

'Dax. She's substituted them for the humans the Dozaurs created. Let's face it, they look so alien no one's memory is likely to be jogged by the sight of Olmukes - apart from ours' of course.'

A deathly silence filled Yuri's living room.

Diana looked at her watch. 'Your soap is on in two minutes Julia,' she said to break it.

The effect was galvanizing. As though the teenager had wings, she took off down the meadow like a like a bird riding a hurricane.

'Well,' Diana smiled nervously. 'Better get back as well.' She turned to Salisbury. 'Would you like to stop the night at my place?'

'He stop here!' snarled Yuri.

Salisbury gave a thin smile at the prospect of spending the night on that lumpy sofa in a strong draught.

CHAPTER 19

The superstrings of entities like Dax and Reniola were spread through several dimensions, which enabled them to escape the indignities Nature made mere mortals endure. To achieve cosmic intelligence they had been ground through Evolution's mill and resented any possibility of being dragged back there. It was inevitable that when two of them were sent to fulfil the commitment made to a species a milliard years before they knew better, complications would arise.

Species surviving for any length of time either burnt themselves out or evolved into something nebulous. Empathising with the mundane reality of lowly mortals could be problematic for anyone who had transcended humdrum evolution and forgotten what it was like. This was the difficulty Dax and Reniola had in understanding corporeal beings with no control over their molecules, and who were stuck in one form for the duration of a brief, rather inconsequential, lifetime until being reincarnated into the next.

However, those who had escaped the rebirth cycle usually had the odd members still fixated on mortal values; the type who wanted to do things for the best, only to end up causing mayhem. This was Dax and Reniola.

Perhaps the Supreme Guardian should have sent the Cosmic Corrector to sort things out in the first place, however catastrophic and against her enlightened reasoning it might have been. Rearranging matter into its basic quantum soup may have been painless for its inhabitants who believed in vengeful gods who did that sort of thing anyway, but enlightened entities were all too aware of the cost to their own integrity. Being one's own judge and jury was a terrible price to pay for their deified state and would mean at least two steps back down that exalted ladder.

The Cosmic Corrector was above such moral judgements. It was a device made of plasma, and served no other purpose than to obey the being unlucky enough to give it orders.

There was only one solution to the Supreme Beings' moral quandary... Hive the problem off to a mortal. That way it would mean only one step back down the ladder of enlightenment. Better still, instruct the Cosmic Corrector make its own choice. It may have been a machine, yet wasn't mindless and didn't get headaches of cosmic proportions.

CHAPTER 20

In the early dawn light, Yuri leaned on his 10 inch reflector to watch the gun party making it way past the radio telescopes to the copse of trees beyond.

He prickled with annoyance. They were supposed to be vegetarians, yet Bert Wheeler, the museum groundsman, Daphne Trotter, and her hunting cronies didn't seem to know that. They had to get up early to shoot things, otherwise the rest of the community would have descended on them for destroying life without a licence. They may have only been after lizards, the only wildlife dim-witted enough to remain on her land, but did not hold a pest controller's authorisation to destroy them.

Yuri pulled on his old corduroy jacket and loaded his ancient starting pistol. The only thing he could do was warn off any creatures that didn't see them coming.

Now totally sober and quite small, he was able to circumnavigate a field of maize without being seen. He arrived on the other side of the copse well ahead of the shooting party and crouched down to wait.

Soon he heard voices.

Yuri took the starting pistol from his pocket, but no one appeared. The shooting party were still too far away to be heard.

As the voices weren't making any sense, he assumed they were in his head. It had to be the cycad juice.

Suddenly a plummy voice above him demanded, 'And what do you think you're doing down there with that gun in your hand?'

Yuri dropped the pistol in fright. Beaming down at him was a dodo.

He toppled back and gawped.

'Well don't just sit there. Either say something or turn into a pumpkin.'

'Reniola!' It couldn't have been anyone else. 'What are you doing in nest talking to yourself?' Yuri took a harder look at the heap of branches and twigs wedged into the fork of the tree. 'It that nest?'

'Well of course it is.' Reniola was obviously pleased with her achievement. 'Took me hours to make, and I never altered so much as one molecule.'

'It does not look very comfortable.'

'Well, it is my first attempt.'

'Perhaps it is better you spend time building nest. Diana, she is not pleased with you or Dax. We do not want Mr Kulp and his friends back here.'

'Oh, don't worry about them. That's only a temporary measure.'

'Until when?'

Reniola stripped another twig and tossed the leaves down. 'Can't rightly say, old thing. Shouldn't be long now.'

There was the sound of footsteps and sotto voices.

'Oh I say,' declared Reniola. 'More visitors. Didn't think this place would be so busy.'

'I thought they were too many to hunt lizards. It is you they come to blast from nest.'

Reniola had to think about this. 'That's not a very sociable thing to do.'

'They are not sociable people, you stupid bird-thing,' hissed Yuri, though should have wondered why he was worrying about a dodo being blasted into its component molecules and merely having its extinct status confirmed.

He retrieved his starting pistol and took cover just as the shooting party appeared.

Reniola peered down quizzically at Bert Wheeler.

'Look! There! There!' he whispered to Daphne Trotter and her followers. 'What did I tell you. Said the thing was nesting up there.'

The gun party was momentarily baffled by the amiably beaky grin and didn't at first register what they were seeing.

'Well, shoot the thing before it flies off,' ordered Daphne Trotter. 'It's not going to sit there forever.'

'Just a moment,' whispered a round man with a moustache. 'I reckon that's a pretty rare bird. Never seen anything like it before.'

'Oh how sweet of you,' squawked Reniola. 'I did make an effort you know.'

The gun party fell back in alarm.

'All I need now is just the right lining for my nest.'

The party below carried on gawping until Daphne Trotter, not one to tolerate insubordination from anything, snapped, 'All right, which one of you learnt to throw his voice?'

Reniola looked about as though also being asked the question.

'Just shoot the bloody thing!' raged Daphne.

'Now that's not a very pleasant attitude to take,' admonished Reniola. 'Especially as I was just about to remark on the marvellous job they made of your new nose.'

That did it.

Daphne put her gun to her shoulder and let the bird have both barrels. There wasn't so much as a ripple in Reniola's molecules; her nest fared less well. It exploded in a hail of twigs and branches which rained down on Yuri.

Automatically, Daphne broke her gun and pushed in more cartridges.

Reniola looked very aggrieved. 'That took me hours to build.'

Yuri could contain himself no longer and burst into laughter.

'I should have known!' exploded Daphne Trotter. 'That bloody man must have been operating it by remote control.'

'Let me give him a good kicking,' insisted Bert Wheeler.

'Now look here,' said Reniola. 'This is going too far.'

Yuri was so paralysed with laughter he wasn't able to get up let alone run off, and only just managed to avoid the blow aimed by the groundsman's boot.

'I'm not going to stand for this, do you hear.' Reniola was sounding more and more like a primary school teacher. 'Yuri may be bad-tempered and rude, but it strikes me you people are much worse.'

'Give him one from us as well, Bert,' rose a chorus of the groundsman's betters. 'Make sure he never comes up here spooking the game again.'

Eventually someone did manage to land Yuri a blow.

Reniola puffed out her feathers and damned the fact she should have been on her best behaviour. A sudden wind swirled about the gun party. It picked them up bodily and carried them across the fields towards Monkton's Mire into which it deposited them, guns and all.

Yuri laughed until he throbbed all over.

'Well I never,' Reniola muttered to herself. 'I thought we had managed to civilise your species a little in bringing them here, but it seems that old ways die hard.' She scowled down at the Russian. 'And you should be ashamed of yourself.'

'Why? Because I do not stay still long enough for them to kill me?' As he saw the group pulling themselves from the distant bog he shouted at them, 'Cossacks!' then fired the starting pistol. 'Peasant murderers! Pheasant murderers!'

'Will you be quiet,' snapped Reniola. 'What are you trying to do? Attract attention?'

This hadn't been Yuri's intention though, given the disguise Reniola had opted for, it seemed odd that she should be concerned about it.

'They will now come to cottage to murder me, you know,' he declared for the record.

'Well don't look at me,' Reniola said huffily. 'We're not supposed to interfere. 'If you hadn't behaved so ridiculously nothing would have happened.'

'They destroy nest after you take so much time over it. You would have put them in mire anyway.'

This was true of course. Reniola settled down in the cleft of the tree to cast him a sideways glance of resentment.

'And that Mr Salisbury is staying with me. What will Diana say if anything happens to him?'

'Oh all right.'

When Yuri got back to his cottage it was surrounded by a twenty foot high pebble dashed wall with access through an automatic gate which demanded fingerprints and iris scans.

When Salisbury woke, he not only had the usual backache, but wondered what had happened to the sun.

He groaned, rolled from the sofa, and hit the threadbare rug with a thud. 'Oh my God. What on earth is that blocking the light?'

The wall outside immediately reduced to ten feet so the sunlight could flood in through the tattered net curtains.

Yuri meandered in as though he had just been for a stroll on some beach.

'What have you been up to?' Salisbury demanded.

'Daphne Trotter and her friends did not want me to play with them.' Yuri dawdled into the kitchen. 'I make tea. You must keep look out for tanks.'

'Oh, I say ...'

'Only joke,' Yuri called from the kitchen. 'How you like toast? Burnt or raw?'

CHAPTER 21

Kulp had filled the secret pockets in his frock with batteries and electrical tools stolen from the supermarket before being stunned and bundled into a security van back to the secure quarters prepared for the human specimens. The guards who had been watching him on a surveillance monitor assumed that the green miscreants were a subspecies of "hoomans" and that their hoarding behaviour was normal.

It had taken some while for security to stop Kulp trying to throttle Jannu and Tolt, so they were separated by transparent screens.

When the lights went down Kulp pulled out the equipment he had concealed in the pockets of the ghastly Salac frock, which also contained the essential components from his lab that he always carried in his oily overalls.

The Olmuke sight was well adapted to the dark, which was just as well because those on his home world had to spend most of their time underground after Kulp had ensured that they would turn bright pink in sunlight.

Jannu and Tolt watched apprehensively all night as he tinkered away with his tools and shoplifted items. Whatever he was up to, they knew it didn't involve rescuing them.

By the morning, before their vegetarian breakfast arrived, Kulp was wearing his usual greasy, grey atmosphere suit and had a blaster tucked in his belt.

He powered up the weapon and melted away the lock of his room. And, to their amazement, he also released Tolt and Jannu.

Kulp had also interfered with the security monitors so their guards did not see them leave.

As the sun rose Kulp blasted an Olmuke-sized hole in the perimeter fence and the three of them stepped out into an unsuspecting world.

'What do you think he's up to?' Tolt whispered to Jannu.

'Not sure. He must have been kidnapped as well.'

'You reckon?'

'Why else would he be escaping?'

'Stop muttering you two and come on!' ordered Kulp. 'Do you want to wait around for Dax to turn up?'

At the mention of her name, Tolt and Jannu hared after him and to the cover of some allotments.

Not being from a farming species, the three Olmuke investigated the tools in the nearest shed as though they could go off at any moment.

Satisfied they were safe enough inside the small room of compost, flower pots and gardening implements, Jannu turned to the others. 'This seems like Earth, but the sky isn't right.'

'Nor were those creatures in the carriages,' added Tolt. 'What happened to them? One moment they looked like humans, the next, like some sort of lizard.'

Jannu shrugged.

Kulp knew that the illusion blinked on and off because it wasn't aimed at them and, lizard or not, he had certainly recognized Diana. Some infernal hand was at work here, and it had to belong to Dax and Reniola. This time they hadn't waited for him to try and exterminate them and got in first. For incompetents, the entities were learning fast. At least the indignity inflicted on Kulp was helping to restore his malicious instincts. He had spent so much time having to be nice to his customers it was beginning to disturb his equilibrium. Rescuing Jannu and Tolt wasn't something he could explain to himself either.

'Now what?' asked Tolt.

'Shut-up!' snapped Kulp. 'I'm thinking.'

'I was in the middle of transporting twenty barges of mineral ore for the New Mott Federation. The Mott females may not be so handy with a blaster when you break a contract, but they can be litigious. There's bound to be some massive forfeit if I don't-'

'Will you shut-up! What do you use for a brain? Those rocks you shunt from planet to planet?'

'Tolt's got a point,' agreed Jannu. 'This whole business is bloody inconvenient. If I don't get back and reprogram those work robots they'll start excavating their way through to the other side of that planet.'

Kulp raised his blaster.

They shut up.

'Right,' Kulp announced. 'We haven't the equipment to open a gravity corridor, so we'll have to improvise.'

CHAPTER 22

'Hi!' shouted Julia. 'Is it your day off?'

Fiona laughed. 'I should be so lucky. Dr Hopkirk believes astronomers should work round the clock. Now we've got the reflector as well as the radio telescopes we have 24 hour rapport with the heavens.'

'Fab.' Julia caught up with the astronomer. 'It must be great being able to look through all those telescopes.'

Fiona wasn't so sure. 'Well, it depends what you

47

find.'

'How do you mean?'

Fiona gave a thin smile and shrugged. 'Just things. Just things.' She changed the subject. 'Where's your mother?'

'I've been to the museum to tell them she won't be in today. No need really, they're pretty used to it.' Julia matched Fiona's stride and suddenly announced, 'I want to be a local government employee when I leave school. Careers officer says it's the best way to guarantee a pension.'

'Aren't you a bit young to make a hard and fast decision about that?'

'But mum said we'll all probably have to work until we're eighty to pay for it anyway.'

Fiona was a logical scientist and the teenager's view of life had a disconcertingly elliptical orbit. 'Do you really want to live to be one hundred?'

'Only if I can still play Pokémon.'

Fiona changed the subject. 'I don't suppose you heard gunfire this morning did you?'

Julia guessed what that must have been about. 'Really? Has Yuri been upsetting Mrs Trotter again?'

'I wouldn't know, but it plays havoc with the telescopes. Just as well Dr Hopkirk never heard. There's some sort of feud going on between her and this Trotter woman.'

'To the death,' enthused Julia. 'They hate each other.'

'Got to admit I agree with Dr Hopkirk. I've never met anyone quite like Mrs Trotter.'

Julia stood stock still. 'Oh look.' She pointed to the path leading past the museum grounds. Coming towards them was a small party of individuals covered from head to toe in glutinous slurry.

'Oh my God, isn't that Bert Wheeler?' exclaimed Fiona.

'AND Mrs Trotter. Take a snap! Quick!'

Julia and Fiona scurried to the cover of the hedgerow. The astronomer pulled out her mobile and recorded the momentous event for posterity as the mud-coated group passed by.

'What's the betting Dr Hopkirk lets me have a couple of days off for these?'

'I bet it's got something to do with Yuri.'

'I didn't think he got up this early?'

'Only if he thinks they're going out to shoot wildlife. Then he scares it off with his old starting pistol.'

'I wonder what happened?'

Julia broke cover to look across to Yuri's cottage. 'That's funny.'

Fiona joined her. 'What is?'

'You can only see part of the roof and the chimney. Looks as though it's surrounded by this high wall.'

'But it wasn't there yesterday?'

'No, it wasn't.' Julia shook her head, then realised. 'Oh no, I thought they must have all been joking.'

'Who? About what?'

'You wouldn't want to know - really.'

The two student workers were ambling up to the museum and saw them staring.

'Hi,' said John.

'Hi,' said Fran.

'Oh, hello.' It was unusual to see the serious Fiona beaming from ear to ear.

'Nice morning,' said John.

'Do they make you start early as well?'

'Got a site to clear. New timber arriving this morning,' explained Fran. 'And,' the student came closer before adding, 'John's been having another of his trips.'

'I have not!' John protested. 'I saw the creatures, I tell you.'

'Honestly, how many large, green, toad-like bipeds are wandering about the area?'

John pointed to Daphne Trotter's shooting party. 'What about them?'

The miserable, mire-sodden group cast resentful looks in the direction of the young people try not to laugh at the sight.

'What about them? However obnoxious, they belong here.'

'I meant, what sort of force could dump those gun-toting thugs into a bog?'

'Why should it be alien?'

'Well, it wasn't likely to be divine retribution for all the lizards they shoot.'

Julia decided to step in. John's state of mind was frequently questioned. She didn't see why. Given the length of beard on one so young, in her judgement he had to be sane.

'Oh, whatever it was, it probably escaped from Brassica Park. That had three green, toad-like things there yesterday. They didn't seem very happy, so they must have got out.'

Then the thunderclap of realisation made the teenager's ears ring. John had a beard! A long beard!

That couldn't be right. They belonged to a species which grew hardly any hair. And the adults around there were behaving more strangely than usual. Had they undergone the same reality attack, and knew what it was all about?

'Are you all right Julia?' asked Fiona.

'Sure, just the shock of getting up so early,' she lied.

'Is your mother ill then?'

'Oh no, not now she's - I mean, she had to go some-where urgently.' Julia turned to leave, and then stopped. 'Oh, I almost forgot. Have you got any more observations for Yuri to see?'

'Plenty, but Dr Hopkirk usually gets to them first.'

'I think Yuri knows what's going on.'

John and Fran looked at each other. This was

astronomy and it was getting too scientific for them, so they made their farewells and went on to the museum.

'Did he say what?'

'Something to do with irregular mass.'

'That would explain the planets' erratic motions.'

'Sounds like diarrhoea.'

It was rather absurd to expect anything more profound from a 13-year-old, so Fiona smiled, retrieved her packed lunch from the hedge and dashed back to the observatory.

CHAPTER 23

Whatever Yuri had been up to at the crack of dawn, it had tired him out and Salisbury was relieved when he went back to bed. As he had no idea where Diana was the scholar decided to pass the time by tidying up the cottage. Yuri wouldn't like it of course, but if he had to spend another night sleeping under several shelves of books that looked as though they could topple onto him at any moment he would lose his mind laying awake waiting for them to fall.

Despite all the hoovering, bumping and thumping going on in the other rooms, Yuri lay wide awake listening to voices in his head. He didn't want to, but had no sensible way of evicting them. At first they didn't make sense, and then he found himself overhearing an extraordinary conversation. As with people on mobile phones discussing personal matters you preferred not to know about, they couldn't be ignored.

There were several individuals in this exchange bickering like adolescents:-

'I don't care if you do have two polar caps; I've five deserts and a girdle of rainforest all the way round my equator.'

'We've heard that a hundred times. Just wait until

an asteroid strikes and alters your rotation.'

'This is an asteroid free zone, you know that.' This voice sounded a little more pompous than the others. 'Our magnetospheres are strong enough to deflect half a dozen comets.'

'Who was asking you?'

'I was getting bored, having to listen to your never-ending drivel.'

'Well, what do you know about it? You're on the other side of the Sun to me.'

'Thank goodness for that.'

'Noticed any interesting solar flares lately?' This voice had a different agenda.

'And if you're going to start going on about your auroral displays-'

'Sorry I spoke.'

'A planet your size shouldn't have a magnetic field that powerful. I reckon you deliberately pinch it in at the poles.'

'I do not! My magnetic field is quite natural.'

'So is my equatorial cloud belt, but I don't make such a fuss over it.'

'Natural indeed! You deliberately adjust your rotation so all the weather systems meet in the middle.'

At this point, the cosmic squabbling sent Yuri's mind into thankful numbness.

Eventually satisfied he would be able to spend another day in the tidier cottage and remain reasonably sane, Salisbury brought him a cup of tea. The astronomer was lying, wide-eyed and motionless on the bed staring at the ceiling as though it was about to fall on him.

CHAPTER 24

Experience had convinced Diana to import from the Dozaur home world a pair of military boots, combat trousers and a jacket with pockets large to carry everything for basic survival. She was still lost without her pink handbag, though. Needing to have both hands free was disconcerting. But Kulp managed it; so would she.

Being the neighbours' principal source of gossip, and not needing them to believe that she was a Dozaur sympathiser as well, Diana left the house before most of them were awake. On a pacifist planet in her combat gear she probably stood out like plesiosaur in the paddling pool. It didn't matter; there was no way she was going to get caught out wearing heels and a tight-fitting skirt in an emergency yet again.

When Diana reached the copse where Reniola had built her nest, the bird was sitting in the fork of the tree, pondering whether to rebuild the chaotic structure. It seemed a waste of time when some bumptious woman and her cronies were bound to come along and blast it to pieces again.

Diana kept out of sight and waited for several hours until she felt herself dozing off in the long grass. If Dax and Reniola were going to meet here, they surely would have done so by now. So why was the dodo reluctant to move? Perhaps she was guarding something? Given her forays away from the action at other inconvenient times, it may not have been important. Or perhaps she was waiting for something else?

Time passed. Diana began to feel hungry and demoralised, so ate a sandwich and drank some water. Julia must have been with her cousins by now; the teenager had learnt to go quietly. Protesting had never done any good and she had even started to enjoy their environmental campaigns before the Earth had started to follow an agenda of its own.

Zoë, her eldest cousin and ringleader of all their ecological enterprises, was 18 going on 58. She was fearsome, focused and so forthright only youths of supreme confidence had dared suggest she should lighten up and join her own age group. But the planet she had known needed to be saved from the older generation destroying it. Zoë disdained those callow, unthinking young men whose worlds existed in selfies taken in perilous situations and behind the wheels of fast cars. Julia, albeit discreetly, admired her campaigning cousin. If she had possessed a fraction of such motivation her mother would have turned cartwheels - when she wasn't saving the Universe, that was. Zoë's younger siblings who sometimes joined her campaigns came from the same mould, though in need of topping up. They had one foot in that obsessive, insecure age group which spent more time chatting on mobiles than to each other. It was small wonder the smartphone had enabled their reality to drift away into a dinosaur dimension.

Diana knew that now Moosevan no longer inhabited the Earth, the pollution was bound to build up again and restore the cousins' reason for existence - assuming they ever managed to return there.

Was watching Reniola going to give her any clue as to how to put things to rights? Despite her doubts, something deep down nagged her to stay where she was.

In the distance people with guns were walking determinedly towards Yuri's cottage. Not to worry, that new security gate wasn't going to let them through in a hurry.

Diana had almost dozed off when something tickled her nose. She opened her eyes to brush it away. Nothing was there. Must have been a blade of grass. She looked up.

Reniola had gone.

'Damn,' Diana cursed.

Now she would have to return home in the full glare of the neighbourhood dressed in ancient army surplus which could only have come from the warlike Dozaur planet. The dratted bird must have known she was spying on her. Reniola could appear so obtuse it was easy to forget that she was from a species so evolved mortality was a novelty they hadn't quite mastered.

If she had to return under the local residents' gimlet glare, she might as well put on her face. This was one of the few occasions she felt bothered about looking her age.

Diana pulled an ancient compact from an inside pocket and powdered her nose.

Something tickled her ear again. She brushed it away, only to be aware of a ribbon of vapour girdling her head.

She quickly turned to see who was smoking.

There was no one about. She should have been used to odd things happening by now, but this was spooky.

Diana got up and searched the small copse to find if the lizards were lighting matches.

The streamers of vapour persisted as though trying to attract her attention.

She had no choice but to address thin air. 'All right, what's going on? Is that you Dax?'

Nothing.

'Reniola?'

Still nothing.

'Dianaaaa...' whispered a low female voice.

'What?' Diana's oft-bleached roots still had enough life left in them to stand on end. 'Who are you?' She pulled herself together. 'Where are you?'

'Where do you want me to be?'

'Where I can see you.'

'What do you want to see?'

55

There had to be a catch. No good at crossword clues, she thought very carefully before answering. Something told her that the wrong reply could traumatise everyone in the region.

'What can you look like?'

'Anything.'

So could Dax and Reniola, but they never asked anyone's opinion before rearranging their molecules.

Whatever the consequences, this was too good an opportunity to miss. 'Do you know what a genie is?'

'Yeeees... Diana.'

'Well something like that, without a moustache or bad temper.'

The air in the copse's small clearing shimmered, and then began to ripple. From the coils of a silvery, serpentine tail a torso bloomed like a pearly tulip. The face had a serene smile that could only have come from Max Factor at his best. This was no lowbrow, pantomime genie performed by a local comedian.

'Well you're certainly no special effect.' Other than that, Diana was unsure what to think. 'You're not Dax or Reniola either. Just who are you?'

'I am the Cosmic Corrector.'

Diana stepped back, expecting to fall through a chink in space-time. 'Oh dear God! You can't be! You shouldn't be here!'

'I am here, therefore this must be.'

'Aren't you some sort of machine? You need someone to operate you?'

'Yeeees...Diana. I must have instructions. I cannot function without them.'

Diana began to wish that she had fallen through a crack in space-time. 'What's that got to do with me?'

'I have selected my operator.'

'No, no, no... Don't tell me!'

But the Cosmic Corrector had made its decision. 'I have selected you... Diana.'

CHAPTER 25

Despite the amount of scrap metal he had handled in his nefarious career, Tolt felt sorry for the automatic taxis Kulp had dismantled for their components.

Jannu was just worried. He knew Kulp's mind better than any other mortal. 'Are you sure this is safe, Kulp? They're searching for us. We're standing out like three quilled demons at a balloon carnival.'

'Stop flapping. I know what I'm doing.'

Something suddenly landed in the branches above them. A confetti of leaves fluttered down as it thudded onto a branch.

'Now, now, boys, what are you up to?'

Swifter than a striking snake, Kulp pulled his weapon and blasted the branch away. Not having time to take off, the dodo flopped down onto the next one. Reniola couldn't understand why no one would take her intergalactic powers seriously in this incarnation.

'Temper, temper.'

'What's the matter with you two do-gooding misfits? the Olmuke raged. 'There's a whole universe out there to torment! Why pick on me?'

'Because it just seems to make such perfect sense.'

Jannu had no time for vitriolic small talk. 'When can we go back? I've got a business to run.'

'Everything is in hand. Don't worry about your business. We only need you here until the Cosmic Corrector turns up.'

'Cosmic Corrector?' demanded Tolt. 'What's a Cosmic Corrector for pity's sake?'

Kulp told him.

The other two Olmuke turned lime green.

'So go and wait somewhere else for it.' Then Kulp realised. 'You're more interested in who's going to give it instructions, aren't you?' he accused the dodo.

'Of course not. It is of no consequence to me whatsoever.'

'It's obviously not going to be either of you two, so you're worried.'

Reniola clattered her huge beak and puffed out her feathers importantly. 'I think you need to be more worried than we are.'

'We haven't done anything to worry about,' Tolt declared confidently.

'Not yet, anyway,' added Kulp.

'Oh,' demanded Reniola. 'And just what have you got in mind?'

Kulp dropped his blaster back into its holster. 'You'll find out soon enough if you don't send us back.'

Reniola didn't believe even he could engineer some worldwide catastrophe with the pile of scrap components he was assembling. 'Oh, you're going to build a gravity tunnel with the pieces from half a dozen auto cabs?'

Tolt believed that was what his partner in crime had been doing. 'Aren't you then, Kulp?' But then, he didn't know any better, even though the engineer's gravity tunnels lacked stabilizers and tended to scramble the molecules before rearranging them back into a reasonably sentient being.

Reniola was no longer listening to them. 'Oh my goodness.'

The incongruous bird once again magically defied gravity and flapped into the air as fast as her clumsy wings would take her. She was soon a disorientated dot on the horizon.

'Why doesn't she just transmit herself there if it's so important?' wondered Jannu.

Kulp knew why. 'Because she's developed a mortality fixation. Wouldn't surprise me if she eventually turns into a traffic controller on some interstellar bypass and forgets how to change back.'

Jannu laughed. 'Then all she need know is how to

decontaminate leaks from the fusion engines of Tolt's garbage fleet and operate a space suction head.'

Tolt wasn't amused. 'That's a highly specialised job, you know. Be disastrous without it.' But then, he had spent most of his life ferrying junk in spaceships that should have joined it at the bottom of some gravitation anomaly.

CHAPTER 26

'What is the matter with you?' Salisbury demanded for the sixth time. He placed the shopping bag on the cracked, marble-topped kitchen table and unpacked it. 'I've got soya marg. Hope that's all right?'

Yuri was lying motionless on the sofa and said nothing, just stared at the ceiling as though having had a flaming row with it.

Salisbury sighed and put the groceries away, all bar a small bottle. He poured the contents into a glass and took it to Yuri. Hardly bothering to raise his head, the astronomer managed to swallow the drink without spilling any.

After a few moments the concoction kicked in. 'What is this?'

'Malted stimulant of some sort. One of the masters swears by it. Drinks at least four before giving a tricky lecture. Obviously works.'

Yuri sat up. 'What is time?'

'Almost two.'

'I must see Diana.'

'She left a note on the back door to say she wouldn't be there and Julia's been sent to her cousins'.'

'That is not good.'

'Why not?'

'Whenever Julia is sent to cousins', things happen.'

'Well let's start with you instead then. How often

59

does your brain shut down without bothering to tell your eyelids?' The schoolmasterly tone had more effect than the voice of sweet reason Salisbury had given up trying to use on Yuri long ago.

'This I cannot explain.'

'Or don't want to.'

'I listen to nightmare.'

'With your eyes wide open?'

'It is someone else's nightmare.'

Before the minutiae of Yuri's delusion could be unravelled there was a loud report outside and splintering of wood.

Salisbury strode over to the window. 'Someone has just shot Reniola's thug proof gate off its hinges.'

'Probably thug.'

'Pity she didn't leave us a back way out. Shall I call the police?'

'There is no need. One of Daphne Trotter's shooting party is chief police inspector.'

'Perhaps they've come to arrest you?'

'I think it more likely they come to murder me.'

There was an almighty thud as the huge gate crashed to the ground.

'They're through. Shall I let them in?'

'Of course. Why not make them cucumber sandwiches and Early Grey tea?'

'They don't look very happy.'

'They have probably just paid dry cleaning bill.' Yuri made a serious effort to get to his feet. 'You should hide. It is only me they want to kill.'

Salisbury may have been a gangling, middle-aged academic who didn't know one end of a cricket bat from the other, but he wasn't a coward. 'I say - we may have our differences, but I'm not going to disappear while you get shot.'

'If I am shot, it will hardly make difference to cosmic order of things, Mr Grammar Teacher.'

'Look Yuri, this is serious!'

There was a vigorous hammering at the door.

'I will answer it,' Yuri insisted.

'But...?'

'Sit down and look English.' Yuri tossed Salisbury his newspaper.

Hardly up to tackling the crossword at that moment, Salisbury listened intently to what was going on in the hall. The lack of raised voices made him even more nervous. Without warning a large, middle-aged man burst in, followed by Bert Wheeler and Daphne Trotter.

They all carried shotguns.

Yuri warily followed them.

Daphne Trotter stopped dead at the sight of the English don. 'Who are you?' she demanded.

'My name is Dr Salisbury. I have taken a couple of days off from my college to see my friend,' he said as though reading the morning service. 'May I ask who you are, Madam?'

To produce a tone that icy, Yuri fancied his companion must have spent time in Siberia.

Unfortunately the woman was too full of her own self-importance to be intimidated by anything from the frozen wastes of any planet. 'This is nothing to do with you. I suggest you leave.'

'I certainly shall not.'

'That is good idea,' nodded Yuri. 'And this lady does not have many.'

The Don stood up his full, gratifying height, and towered over the intruders. 'Just what is going on?'

'It's all right Sir,' the large man assured him. 'Nothing is going to happen.'

'Well in that case, I see no reason why I shouldn't stay.' Salisbury sat down and returned to his newspaper.

Yuri shrugged coyly. 'Now Mrs Trotter, how can we

help you?'

'Don't play the innocent with me.'

'Perhaps you wish to pay for damage to gate?'

'Just step outside.'

'No thank you. I have seen outside today.'

Salisbury peered over the top of his newspaper. 'Threatening people with guns is not very sensible.'

'And what do you intend to do about it?' snarled Bert Wheeler.

Until then, Salisbury had hoped they only intended to frighten Yuri. Now he realised they could get away with grievous bodily harm. His testimony to the magistrate, who was probably in the Trotter family's pocket, would count for nothing. Then he remembered seeing something in the kitchen. Though it had been dusty and never used, he knew what it was for. He got up and nonchalantly strode across the room.

'Keep away from the phone,' snapped the middle-aged man.

Salisbury sighed in tedium. 'There is no phone in the kitchen. And I think you'll find that the one in here is out of order.'

As Salisbury passed them, he lifted the receiver. 'Not working, and believe me, I have never had the inclination to carry a mobile phone. I take it you won't be staying for tea?'

Daphne Trotter indicated the kitchen door. 'Don't let him back in.'

After he had gone Bert Wheeler jammed a chair under the handle.

'So now you shoot me,' shrugged Yuri. 'Lady Empress of all she surveys achieves her ambition at last.'

'No, we're not going to shoot you.' The large man swung his gun round and showed Yuri the stock. This didn't look any more promising.

Yuri leapt over the sofa and snatched away some

fire tongs supporting an overloaded shelf. Several heavy volumes and a bust of Galileo crashed to the floor.

'If that's the way you want it!'

'No, this is way you want it! You are sort of stupid people who used to burn scientists who did not agree with them! You want to run planet, Mrs Trotter, but planet is not interested in what you want.'

'How did you set up that ambush in the copse?'

'I set up nothing. What were you there shooting anyway?'

'That's none of your business.'

Bert Wheeler lunged at Yuri and clipped his shoulder with the stock of his gun. Yuri lashed out with the tongs and, considering how short his arms were, made a respectable gash across the man's face.

Then all hell let loose.

Yuri was on home territory and tipped over furniture, hurled bottles hidden in corners where Salisbury had not been able to find them and, having a very good set of teeth for his age, bit any part of their anatomy that came within range.

Believing murder was being done, Salisbury hammered at the kitchen door, unable to budge the chair.

Winded and bruised by the blows that did land, Yuri still had the energy to seize the foam extinguisher Eva had insisted he keep, and expel its contents over the despicable Daphne Trotter. The sight of the enraged snow woman sent Yuri into hysterical laughter and gave her companions the chance to seize him.

Daphne raised the butt of her shotgun and showed every intention of smashing it into his face.

'Don't mark him where it shows,' warned the middle-aged man.

Daphne was beyond worrying about such niceties and the weapon was already travelling when there was a hollow, dull report from the hall doorway.

Daphne Trotter's scarf was whirled into a knot by

the impact that spun the gun from her hands. To make sure they got the message, another dull report, and a hole was blown through the plasterboard kitchen wall, giving Salisbury the fright of his life.

What manner of creature could fire a weapon like that and not be spread thinly across the adjoining meadow by its recoil?

'I warned you about trespassing on my property, Mrs Hole-in-the-knickers,' snarled Dr Eva Hopkirk. 'Now, do you want to see what colour your own evil brain is, or do I just kneecap you from the neck down?'

Neither of the men had encountered a weapon like that before and dropped Yuri. No longer having anything to wield, Daphne Trotter backed away.

'What the hell is that thing!'

'Astronomer's best friend.' Eva gave a wicked smile. 'It's all right; I've got a licence for it. With you and your crowd of psychopaths roaming the area at all times of night, the observatory needs protection.'

The men followed Daphne towards the door.

'Leave the guns!'

The three intruders obeyed and edged out of the room.

Just as Salisbury managed to break through the hole in the wall of the kitchen, Yuri lost the feeling in his knees and crumpled to the floor.

Seeing only fire extinguisher foam and hardly any blood, the scholar sank to a chair in relief. 'My goodness, you were quick.'

'He's never used the panic button when he was in trouble before, so I knew it had to be serious.'

Salisbury hauled Yuri onto the sofa. He patted his cheeks, but the astronomer was quite comatose. 'On no, not again.'

Eva placed her pump-action shotgun on the table. What's the matter?'

'He's been having these... fits. Just lays there, eyes

open, apparently asleep.'

'Well, at least it keeps him away from the cycad juice.'

'And Diana's disappeared.'

'Oh good. Fiona said something about her having the day off.'

'Good? What can we do without her? And what if those lunatics come back?'

'Don't worry about them. I'll electrify the perimeter.'

'That's illegal.'

'So's the pump-action shotgun, but I can't see the Trotter gang raising the matter in court.'

'Oh honestly.'

'You are having a rotten reality attack, aren't you?'

'I'm sorry, but now I know that this is an illusion, it's beginning to give me the horrors.'

'In that case, both of you had better come up to the observatory where I can keep an eye on you. There's plenty of room and no draughts.'

It sounded like a good idea to Salisbury. 'All right. What about Yuri? He's out cold.'

'Wait till he comes round. Better to move both of you when it's dark, just in case.'

Neither of them could tell if Yuri knew what they were talking about. He just lay there, motionless, staring at the ceiling and listening to voices saying:-

'Just what is wrong with your orbit? Have you been struck by an asteroid?'

'Not so much as a meteor. There are no pock marks on me. You're the one who's started to become wonky.'

'Will you two stop arguing. There is something wrong. I can feel it. My axis has tipped at least five degrees.'

'Yes, I can feel it as well. I haven't got enough mass to keep this up much longer.'

'Keep what up for goodness sake?'

'I'm losing momentum and feel as though I'm falling.'

'Don't be absurd. You're in space. Where can you fall to?'

'Oh, they're just anxiety attacks. Be telling us you're afraid of heights next.'

'Well, just look at my oceans will you, and the height of my tides - and I haven't even got a moon. Something is definitely pulling at me, I tell you.'

'Well, does it matter as long as you don't collide with me.'

'And I think I'm shrinking.'

'Oh, for pity's sake.'

CHAPTER 27

Tacal Tehalt snarled at the message on his monitor. What was the Olmuke thinking of, setting up a tourist industry that progressive, yet having no one to take bookings, let alone return calls? All the Kleet had managed to contact was an inaudible Dringle who was only interested in customer parking and Kulp's androids who were programmed to cyber secrecy.

Tacal Tehalt had it all, and most of it once belonged to the Mott Empire. Now he wanted the ultimate prize. And only Kulp had that. The difficulty would be persuading the Olmuke to part with his brain. He would have been happier to stay where Dax and Reniola had put him had he known what the multi-trillionare was planning, even for a tempting down payment. But the bloated, ginger Kleet had the ruthlessness of the Mott, yet was also cunning; something the Mott had always left to their androids - with disastrous consequences.

Many of the planets which had been under the heel of Mott domination were now in thrall to Tacal Tehalt's bank for loans they would have refused to take out if he had not blackmailed them with an embargo on trade. Even the Mott females had difficulty in charitably redistributing the wealth of their mates' old empire after the shock troopers of the new mercantile order, posing as concerned entrepreneurs, had bought up the other planets. This was asset-stripping on a cosmic scale.

The altruistic plans of Gilli Gott and her android, Toc, had been swamped by the new wave of corruption sweeping the galaxy. The surge was so high it seemed inevitable that the galaxy's dwindling collection of star clusters, supernovae remnants, and red giants would gutter out in a miserable pool of criminality. But Gilli was not a Mott to give up. She had survived the worst excesses the males of her species could throw at their mates, surreptitiously studying engineering, astrophysics, chemistry, economics and domestic science. Even though she was a match for Tacal Tehalt, it was unlikely she could reach him. The bloated Kleet was too well embedded in his own security web and only met people he could do business with.

Not all of them left in one piece.

Gilli didn't know that Tacal was searching for Kulp. She was aware of the Olmuke's reputation but wasn't intimidated by it, though she might have reviewed her opinion if she found out that the engineer was about to blow up a planet.

CHAPTER 28

The jumble of components hummed, blinked and made sinister whirring sounds.

Kulp seemed pleased with his handiwork and Tolt and Jannu knew better than to regard it as a pile of junk.

'You'd think somebody would be wondering what had happened to all those auto cabs,' observed Tolt.

'Shut up!' hissed Jannu.

Being a total stranger to the empathic nature of mortal beings, Kulp was in the only reverie he knew... the worship of his own genius and the wonders it could create from the pathetic technology of lesser intellects. He fondly stroked the only casing that didn't have a million volts running through it, and the machine responded as though recognising its master by throwing off enough luminosity to signal satellites.

To the impatient Jannu, this could only mean one thing. 'Is the wave gun ready for a trial run now?'

'Not yet you fool!' snapped Kulp. 'They have to think it's a natural earthquake. We need to be well away from its epicentre when I trigger it.'

Tolt was beginning to miss the other sort of disasters that Dax and Reniola engineered. At least they meant well when rearranging the solar system and creating havoc with its timelines.

'Why do you think Dax and Reniola haven't bothered with us for so long?'

Kulp knew. 'Something else is going on. They're too busy watching their own backs.'

'Think we should know about it?'

'No. We only need them to turn up when it matters.'

'So they can blast us into the fifth dimension when they realise what we're doing.' For such a bumbling idiot, Tolt could often have an accurate grasp of what fate was liable to throw at them.

CHAPTER 29

Fiona laid her observations on the table in front of Yuri. 'These were made two nights ago.'

Salisbury grimaced. Graphs were just mathematics to him.

There was no pattern to the movements as far as Yuri could make out. They would need to take more readings for that to become apparent. He shouldn't have been surprised. The mass of all those small worlds was wrong to begin with, and how could they have all been formed in the same orbit?

Eva darted a warning glance across the observatory canteen and Yuri thought better of telling Fiona the truth.

So he shrugged. 'Perhaps instability was caused by close pass of asteroid creating a chain reaction.'

Fiona looked at him as though he was a benevolent - quite mad - uncle.

'Damn,' cursed Eva. 'I forgot to program the array.'

'Plenty of time,' said Fiona. 'It's only midnight and has another twenty four hours to run.'

'All the same, could you see to it?'

Fiona leapt up enthusiastically. 'Of course.' This wasn't something she was usually allowed to do without the senior astronomer looking over her shoulder.

As soon as Fiona had left, Eva turned on Yuri, 'Will you be more careful, I don't want the girl caught up in this as well. If she lives long enough she'll make a half-decent astronomer - assuming everything out there is put back in the right place in the not too distant future.'

'Do you think we ought to phone Diana?' asked Salisbury.

'She'd have called Yuri if she wanted us.'

'His phone is out of order.'

Eva leapt up. 'Why didn't you tell me?' She dashed to the observatory kiosk in the hall. Although Dr Hopkirk knew everything there was to know about electromagnetic radiation, she was another member of the intelligencia with a phobia about putting a mobile phone to her ear.

She dialled out. It rang about eight times before being picked up.

'Hallo?' said a yawn.

'Diana, just making sure you're all right?'

'Of course I'm all right. I'd be even better if you hadn't woke me up.'

'That's fine then. But I think you should know that Tilly Trotter and her gang are on the warpath. They tried to kill Yuri.'

'What for? Anything special, or just thinning out the wildlife again?'

'Something about him using a large bird to take the piss out of them. You'll have to work it out for yourself.'

'You haven't left him and Salisbury alone?'

'They're with me at the observatory.'

'Lot of glass up there.'

'That's the least of our problems. Fiona's observations now seem to be saying that all the planets in our orbit are starting to wobble.'

'Wobble? What does Yuri make of it?'

'He's not saying, but I'm convinced the whole system is unstable.'

'And if you're right?'

'Planets will start to collide.'

'Is that bad?'

'Wake-up woman! When planets collide, they don't bounce. What have you been doing all day anyway?'

'Oh hell, now there's someone at the door.'

'Don't answer it!'

'It could be Cherry's twins. Their mother might have gone into labour.'

'No it isn't! Don't answer it!'

'Hold on.'

Eva heard the phone being laid aside. 'Diana!!' She listened intently to the distant conversation.

Those needle-sharp tones couldn't have belonged to anyone but Daphne Trotter.

'Hello Diana. Sorry to disturb you.'

Diana obviously didn't believe it for a minute. 'Hello Daphne, why the crowd behind you? It's a bit early for carol singing isn't it?'

'Just wanted to know if you've seen Yuri?'

'Yes thanks, I've often seen Yuri.'

'I meant, do you know where he is now?'

'He's not at home then?'

'No, but I'm sure you know where he is.'

'Well he's not here, and I've got a feeling I shouldn't tell you even if I did know.'

'Then I can only think of one other place he might be.'

'And where's that?'

'The observatory of course.'

'Might not be a good idea to disturb Dr Hopkirk, you know what she can be like.'

'Oh yes, that's why I've got these plain clothes police officers with me.'

'Really? What has she been up to then?'

A male voice cut in. 'She removed a firearm from the premises it was licensed for, and discharged it with intent to main or kill.'

'Goodness, I wonder why?' observed Diana sarcastically.

There was a pause. Something had apparently caught Daphne's eye. 'What are those Dozaur battle fatigues doing on the banisters, Diana?'

'Too tired to hang them up.'

'Who do they belong to?'

'I don't suppose you keep firearms in the house, Madam?' asked another policeman.

'What on Earth - I mean - why should I? Who in this neighbourhood is liable to break down my front door and try to smash my face in with the butt of her shotgun?'

Eva was puzzled. She hadn't said anything to her friend about that.

Diana yawned. 'I think I ought to come up to the observatory with you.'

'There will be no need Marm.'

'Eva is a friend of mine. She might not take a pot shot at me.'

'And we would appreciate if you didn't warn her that we are on the way.'

'Not a word shall pass my lips. Good night.'

The door slammed.

Diana picked up the receiver. 'Hi-de-hi! Playtime!'

'Not funny,' snarled Eva. 'Now I've got to move everyone again.'

'I've got a better idea.'

'Like what?'

'As there are few places you could get them to in time, and it would be a devil of a job for you to break into the museum grounds, even if you could persuade Salisbury to bunk down in some draughty medieval mock-up, I think we ought to go to the root cause of all this trouble.'

'I know I should have shot the woman when I had the chance.'

'Oh what's the use! Go and drink your Ovaltine. You probably won't get any in the local cop shop.'

Diana ended the call and went into the living room. She sat down in an armchair and gazed intently at the bamboo plant stand Salisbury had sent her for Christmas. As every pot plant she had brought into her house either died or attracted whitefly, it just took up valuable space, but it was the thought that counted. Though, with Salisbury, she had no way of guessing what it was. The man was a veritable labyrinth of complexes.

Fortunately the cars outside were still being choked into life on the thin mix that now passed for petrol, so it gave her time to concentrate her thoughts before they became swamped with images of her gun-toting friend blowing away the most obnoxious creature in the district. After the long communications Diana had achieved with Moosevan, the planet dweller, she had now got the hang of it, though it wasn't easy when this subject wasn't so willing.

Slowly, fuzzily, the shape of a dodo appeared. It was perched precariously on the plant stand.

Reniola looked surprised. She hadn't intended to come here. In fact she thought she had comfortably roosted for the night.

'Now look here,' she began to bluster.

'Shut-up!'

'How did you do that? Wasn't Dax was it? What is she up to now? I had just got settled.'

'Close the beak and engage the brain.'

The beak clattered shut.

'You almost got Yuri killed,' Diana accused. 'Eva stopped it, so there are going to be coppers swarming all over her observatory. At this moment in time it would not be convenient for any of us to be arrested. Have you got that? Nod if you understand me.'

Reniola nodded.

'Now, it is your turn to do something useful, and I don't mean building a fifty foot wall round the observatory. Do you understand?'

Reniola nodded - she wasn't sure why. She was supposed to be the intergalactic intelligence.

'Now go.'

No longer held in Diana's mental traction beam, the dodo blinked from sight.

CHAPTER 30

Deep in the cave even potholers avoided, Kulp threw one of the switches on his patchwork control panel.

Jannu and Tolt apprehensively watched the seismometer. The needle didn't move for some while. Then gradually tremors rippled the planet's crust. Within a 15 mile radius barns were turned into matchsticks, and several lakes slopped over their banks.

Kulp had expected more impressive results. 'Damn,

that's hardly going to attract much attention.'

'Better not kill anyone, Kulp. You know what Dax and Reniola will do,' warned Jannu, backing as close as he dare to the rim of the ledge out of Kulp's reach. He risked plummeting over a thousand feet and double-checked his safety harness just in case.

Naturally Tolt had to embroider the observation. 'Yes. They might not send us back.'

'Not in one piece anyway,' muttered Jannu.

'You spineless blobs!' But Kulp knew they were right. At this rate, the super entities wouldn't even realise anything was happening. Just how far did he need to go to attract their attention? They were on a planet smaller than Earth, the mantle was much denser and any fault lines tended to slide past each other as though lubricated by WD40. He needed to make a deeper fault in the crust where the stress would rapidly build.

'Hello Kulp.'

The three Olmuke froze. They weren't prepared for Dax's appearance just yet.

But it wasn't her. Although the voice was familiar, no indigenous inhabitant of the planet could know how to speak their language.

The three of them looked up to see a woman far above in the entrance of the cave.

'Sorry to disturb you boys.'

Kulp lost his balance in surprise and knocked Tolt off the ledge from where he dangled over the subter-ranean abyss on his safety line.

'Diana?' Until then, Kulp hadn't been sure how the name was pronounced as he had only ever heard it in human.

'Mind if I come down?'

Kulp didn't answer. He was too busy trying to work out why they could understand each other. On the cosmic scale of evolutionary diversity, it shouldn't have been possible.

Diana lightly sprang down like a mountain goat from rock to rock to join them. This was not normal for a middle-aged woman with encroaching arthritis.

'Bit damp down here. Wouldn't you prefer doing something more suited to your talents than trying to judder about a small planet in the back of beyond?'

Kulp braced himself. 'What do you mean?' He wasn't too sure he wanted to know. The situations he had previously found himself in when encountering this particular female still gave him nightmares.

'You are aware things are getting out of hand back in your galaxy, aren't you?'

'It's always been chaotic there. That's the way our galaxy works.'

'Might be something you can do about it.'

Kulp doubted that, even for an arch-villain with his criminal abilities. 'Where are Dax and Reniola?'

'Too busy to bother about you. Probably won't get round to sending you back for some time. So think about the offer. 'Oh -' Diana indicated Kulp's tremor-inducing equipment. 'Don't do that.'

Without warning it melted into an odd smelling puddle.

'I'll be back. Stay good.'

And she was gone.

CHAPTER 31

Dax was once again confronting the consequences of her last efforts to put things right in this corner of space.

It shouldn't have been happening.

As soon as she had pushed one planet back into a stable orbit, another would rapidly start to tilt like a badly pivoted top about to describe an erratic ellipse on the cosmic carpet. Given the speed with which the necklace of moons, planetoids and planets had been crowded into a single orbit to accommodate the offspring created when Moosevan divided, it was hardly surprising. Lots of little planet dwellers now had immature whims of their own. Erratic behaviour should have been expected.

Dax daren't push any of the worlds into different orbits for fear of their ecosystems either freezing or boiling away. No wonder the Supreme Guardian was annoyed.

To make matters worse, none of the fledgling planet dwellers would talk to her - which was only to be expected. Moosevan had refused to do so as well.

The planet dwellers continued to gossip amongst themselves, and apparently to someone else, but not to Dax.

There was nothing to be done until she found out what was wrong.

CHAPTER 32

Salisbury and Yuri were safely locked in the observatory kitchen and Fiona was too busy programming the telescope schedules to notice Eva stride out to meet the approaching unmarked police cars.

The astronomer experienced the thrill of impending combat as she recognised the expensively remoulded profile of her own personal Aunt Sally.

As a reptile, she looked even more ludicrous.

'Well, well, Lady Muck in moonlight. Was that luminous glow part of the cosmetic package or just down to ultraviolet stitches?'

'Don't talk to me in that manner, you contemptible little nonentity!' Daphne snapped as though Eva might have paid the slightest bit of attention.

The local tyrant's law enforcement lackeys leapt out to join her.

'My, my, doesn't a private education work wonders.'

Eva turned to the police officers. 'She can probably spell "false accusation" as well.'

'Dr Hopkirk, are you aware of the complaint that has been made against you?' declared the senior officer.

'Which one? Over the years she's thought up quite a few.'

'I understand you removed a firearm from these premises with the intent of attempting to murder or maim Mrs Trotter?'

'Goodness no. If I'd meant it she wouldn't be around now to make any complaint.'

'Nevertheless, you do not deny it?'

'She was about to smash in my husband's face with the butt of her shotgun and the assistance of two accomplices. As I am not a black belt at karate, I merely used reasonable force to prevent it.'

'Are you denying the charge?'

'I am telling you that I acted on my husband's behalf. They had broken into his home with the intention of doing him grievous bodily harm.'

'That's a lie!' Daphne declared so loudly the radio telescopes must have registered the outburst.

'Then what were you doing in his home? Making up a bridge party?'

'I think you had better come down to the station with us, Dr Hopkirk,' ordered the policeman.

'The station? I thought that had been turned into a pottery?'

'The county station.'

'So that's where the reinforcements have come from. Must be serious to bring them all the way out here.'

'Attempted murder is a serious matter.'

'Then why not arrest Madam tight-ass?'

'That's not why we're here.'

'Oh no, of course not. A foreign refugee like Yuri deserves to be beaten up every now and then. This must all be very time-consuming for you, Inspector. I'm sure you need every spare minute to lick all the boots necessary for promotion.'

'There's no call for that attitude.'

'As I'm being wrongfully arrested, I think there is all the call in the world for it.'

'Please get in the car.'

In the distance came a frantic call. Yuri had just managed to scramble through the kitchen window. 'Eva! Do not go! You cannot trust them!'

As the others had not heard and matters would be far worse if he was arrested as well, Eva stepped into the car, which immediately drove away.

Her husband ran as fast as he could after them, but the toll of consuming so much cycad juice took its toll and he was soon gasping for air.

Salisbury caught up with him. 'Oh my God. Now what?'

'You know influential people?'

'Not in the police. I've made an art of steering clear of them, and the only lawyers I know are clinically unstable.' Salisbury hesitated. 'You don't really think they'll harm her, do you?'

'Why else they take her away? They would not dare let charges come to big court.'

'High court.'

'Whether it is down here or up there, it does not matter!' Yuri began to beat his forehead and turn circles in frustration. 'We must do something!'

Salisbury seized his wrists. 'Will you stop that. It's not doing any good.'

'You do not understand.'

'You've always told me you don't like the woman.'

'What has this to do with love? And Diana will never forgive me. Eva was her best friend.'

'She's not dead yet.'

'Where is car?'

'Several streets back from Diana's.'

'That is too far.'

'You didn't think I would park it outside her front door did you? And what good would it do chasing them? They could be anywhere by now if they're not going back to the station.'

'You should not have pushed panic button!'

'You would be minus a face. Even on you, that would not have been an improvement. Come back inside. We'll phone the regional police HQ to see if they know anything about this, and then we'll have to find a solicitor.'

'Solicitor! Solicitor! Eva is about to be murdered and he talks about solicitors! This man does not live in real world!'

'Nor does anyone else at the moment.' Salisbury eased Yuri back inside. 'We'd better think of something to tell Fiona.'

CHAPTER 33

Tacal Tehalt's powerful grip pulled the messenger robot closer.

Not used to seeing mortals eyeball to eyeball, it was disorientating for a machine programmed to avoid coming into close contact with any corporeal being.

'That's the eleventh time you've brought me this message?' snarled Tacal.

As though surprised that the trillionare tyrant could count up to ten, the robot clunked a few gears before coming up with a credible response. 'That is because the astrascope keeps telling me to bring them.'

'Why hasn't it managed to track that Olmuke yet? It's the most advanced tracking system in the galaxy and it can't find a greasy, paranoid, smelly Olmuke?'

Not holding that much store by body odours itself,

the messenger robot was more sensitive to rough handling, and shuffled its way out of Tacal's grasp.
'Perhaps he is no longer in this galaxy.'

Tacal thudded back down onto his cushion and his gelatinous, ginger midriffs juddered. Not in this galaxy? There were no other galaxies, only a faint glimmering on the infrared scanners of the deep space telescopes the Mott hadn't plundered for their parts. How could Kulp not be in this galaxy?

If the Mott androids hadn't been infected by delusions of grandeur they might have worked out why it was receding into nothingness.

Unfortunately, thinking was no longer at a premium in this corner of desolated space.

CHAPTER 34

The leading car, with Eva being guarded in the back seat and the gloating Daphne beside the driver, turned into an unlit lane.

'Taking the scenic route?' inquired the astronomer.

'Keep quiet,' ordered Daphne.

There was a very nasty drop up ahead and the hazard lights the council had installed were no longer working. Cars always risked swerving off it in the pitch darkness.

Eva's abductors obviously didn't have the nerve to shoot her. As for Yuri; who was going to take his word for anything? And Salisbury had even more reason to keep clear of the authorities after the army discovered aliens in his garden.

The odd copper could be bought off - but all three at once? It must have cost Daphne Trotter a packet to get them to do the dirty work for her. The astronomer should have been flattered that the woman thought she was worth it.

Then, for a second, reality blinked as though an oncoming lorry had flashed its headlights and then sped off.

'There is something you ought to know,' Eva suddenly announced.

Daphne was thrown for a moment by her change of tone. 'What?'

'This isn't real.'

The policeman guarding Eva looked apprehensive. 'What's she on about?'

'I'm talking about realities, and the way they can be slightly adjusted to weaken a person's judgement.'

He eased away as though she still had the pump-action shotgun under her overalls.

'Now take Lady Macbeth here,' Eva went on, 'in the real world she'd just be your ordinary, stuck-up local tyrant, but here... because everyone is so placid, nobody stands up to her and she does just as she likes. In the real world, you wouldn't allow it, let alone join in. The thought of several years in Holloway or Wormwood Scrubs would soon make all of you slam the brakes on.'

The driver laughed nervously. 'What are you waffling on about, woman?'

'Well, it's like this - I'm trying to say that things aren't always what they seem.'

It crossed Daphne's mind that this was nothing like the Dr Eva Hopkirk she had spent so much time despising.

There was an edge of panic in her voice as she ordered, 'Next turning on the left.'

'Oh, it's much further than that,' chuckled their prisoner in a very un-Eva like way.

'You don't know where we're going Dr Hopkirk!' snapped Daphne.

'Oh but I do.'

There was a sharp cry from the policeman in the back seat.

He undid his safety belt and leapt from the moving car.

Daphne spun round.

Sitting where Eva had been seconds before, smiling serenely at her, was a huge dodo.

'What the hell!!'

'Don't look at me. I never pushed him,' said Reniola. 'Must have had something on his mind.'

'Stop the car!'

The driver stamped on the brake. Nothing happened.

'I can't open the door,' wailed Daphne.

'Don't panic.' The driver tried to call up the following car. There was no response.

Reniola beamed. 'Hope you don't get car sick. You're going to be in this one for several hours - going round and round and round. Now, if you'll excuse me, must fly.'

With that, the preposterous bird disappeared.

CHAPTER 35

Kulp had no idea how he had arrived in this luxurious, yet slightly cluttered, chamber. The air was filled with a heady perfume that overpowered his Olmuke olfactory senses more used to toxic lubricants and body odours verging on decomposition. At least Jannu and Tolt weren't there. The last he saw of those two they were sulking in a dank, dark subterranean cave. Dax couldn't have been responsible this time. Whenever she shunted his molecules about it felt as though it had been with hobnail boots.

Kulp remained where he was, stretched out on a mattress which moulded itself to his portly Olmuke dimensions.

In the half-light, something glimmered. It was a

Mott android.

Most of those machines had been destroyed and he couldn't think of any reason why he should trust the few that remained. Kulp no longer had his blaster and it looked as though he would have to do the very thing he spent a lifetime avoiding, and negotiate.

The android faintly clicked as it approached the Olmuke. 'Oh don't worry about me. I'm quite tame - unless you want to be unpleasant of course. I'm sure you're far too civilised for that.'

'Where am I?'

'Back in your own beautiful galaxy, where else.'

Kulp leapt up. 'What about my-'

'Star cruisers? Don't worry about them. Gilli Gott has ensured the passengers know nothing and that business will carry on as usual.'

'How?'

'I am able to communicate quite well with your robots. It was interesting to discover that you based their construction on the Mott model.'

That was because they were the best spare parts Kulp could get, and he wasn't going to admit to the self-assured unit that it was due to expediency.

'What am I doing here?' he snarled.

'Being hidden from the gentle attentions of Tacal Tehalt.'

The Olmuke knew that name all too well. 'What does he want with me?'

Then he remembered the muddled message from the Dringle only interested in customer parking. That personality-deprived trillionare had an only interest in one part of him, and the prospect disorientated even his hardened criminal sensitivities. Obnoxious as Kulp was, having his brain transplanted into an artificial body Tacal Tehalt could command would hardly be an improvement.

'Don't worry,' the android assured Kulp in a manner a little too syrupy for a machine, or comfort. 'You're quite safe here - for now. The astrascope cannot penetrate these walls - well, not easily anyway. My name is Toc, by the way.'

But Kulp wasn't listening. 'I can't stay here forever, wherever it is.'

'We don't intend you to, but first we'll have to get down to business.'

'With Gilli Gott?'

'Of course.'

'I don't do business with namby-pamby do-gooders.'

'That's all right by us. Be a waste, but if you'd really like Tacal Tehalt to fillet your skull we'll not stand in your way. Us namby-pamby do-gooders never thrust our charity onto those who do not want it.'

Toc had a point.

'And what's Gilli Gott's price for preventing it?'

Without warning, the android had such a plausible panic attack, it was a wonder its circuits didn't cross-connect.

'Oh dear, there are so many things going on at once! Too much input!'

Kulp briefly had the feeling that something else, powerful, sinister, was in the chamber with them.

'What's the matter with you?'

'You'll have to excuse me.'

'What things are going on?'

A mechanical edge entered Toc's tone. 'You wouldn't believe it.'

Kulp wasn't going to accept that. 'Only Yat, the Mott's prime android, evolved a dishonesty chip, so tell me.'

The android's demeanour changed again and it appeared to lift several inches from the floor in its own bizarre, private ecstasy. 'Something wonderful is about to happen.'

Kulp didn't like the sound of that either. What was wonderful for most other deserving species often involved him being tossed through some unstable singularity or blasted into his molecular components.

'I know Dax and Reniola are back,' he snarled.

'Something more exciting than that.'

Exciting wasn't one of Kulp's favourite expressions either.

'Why can't you tell me?'

'Have you ever considered positron urban renewal? But so many things could go wrong if Tacal Tehalt and his evil forces can't be stopped.'

'Can I get off here?' asked Kulp. 'I hear the bells of social justice ringing.'

'And you are going to be part of it.'

'No thanks, I've got a reputation to live up to.'

Toc faintly clicked as it re-entered its disconcertingly sinister mode. 'Well, let me put it this way. If you can't find it in your heart to help us namby-pamby do-gooders, I'm afraid your reputation is going to be rather posthumous.'

'If it's all the same to you, I'd rather not have any more character building exerci- What did you say?'

'If you refuse to help us, then your sacrifice will be totally wasted.'

Kulp felt his acute sense of self-preservation being crushed by a huge fist - albeit one in a velvet glove.

'What sacrifice?'

CHAPTER 36

Fiona watched anxiously as the computer printed out its calculations. 'This isn't possible.'

Another thing that Eva had learnt from experience was that anything astronomical could often be a matter of opinion. 'What's happening now?'

'The small planets seem to be searching for some centre of gravity.'

'Are we included?'

'Must be. There's no way we could avoid the collision if they decide to accrete.'

Eva cast an experienced eye over the calculations. 'I reckon you're right.'

'But why would they want to do that, Dr Hopkirk?'

'Let's discuss it in a fast car.'

'Fast car?'

'Daphne Trotter is out to arrest me, and probably torch the observatory into the bargain.'

'We can't leave the telescopes at a time like this.'

'I've called in Desmond and his wife to caretake. They wouldn't dare attack an elderly couple... and he knows where I keep the other shotgun. We can brief them over the phone.'

'But..?'

'Get your things together. I don't know how long this will take.'

When Eva reached the rest room Yuri was once again laying stretched out on the couch, eyes wide open and motionless.

'Not again.'

Salisbury had given up trying to bring him round. 'Of all the times to go into a trance. The wretched man can't- 'Then something occurred to him. 'Dr Hopkirk! We saw you being arrested! How did you escape?'

Eva wasn't going to waste time explaining and motioned to Yuri. 'They're probably pretty annoyed about it. Can you get him into the car?'

'What happened?'

Then Salisbury saw the huge dodo perched on top of the open door.

It had to duck to avoid the ceiling. 'Sorry about that.'

All he could do was wonder why an extinct bird could speak in a disconcertingly plummy accent. It reminded him of an old college matron.

'This is getting bloody silly.'

The dodo fluffed out its feathers, reluctant to admit that Daphne and friends had escaped. She should have made the cars go faster, but had been afraid of causing an accident. How could she have known they would to shoot the locks off the doors and jump out to phone for reinforcements? Calls must have now gone out for the arrest of a desperate astronomer armed with a pump-action shotgun and her parrot.

'Reniola!' snapped Salisbury when he realised what had happened. 'You had better get us out of this pretty quick!'

'Oh, so that's one of the super-turnip heads is it?' said Eva. 'I should have known.'

The dodo's feathers bristled. 'There's no need for that. You would be in pieces at the bottom of the cliff if I hadn't turned up.'

'Well look here, dicky bird, there's something else you'd better start bothering about.'

Reniola wasn't going to give the bad-tempered woman the satisfaction of making her admit she had got something else wrong as well and refused to take the bait.

But Eva knew who was responsible. 'All the planets in this orbit have found their common centre of gravity and are showing a strong inclination to collide.'

'And why can't I bring Yuri round?' demanded Salisbury.

Reniola peered down at the comatose Russian and immediately realised what had happened to him. 'Oh goodness, why didn't we think of that?'

'Think of what?'

'He's still in contact with Moosevan.'

'He can't be, she divided into umpteen smaller planet dwellers. After she swallowed Krykal, the lightning entity, her mass increased to the point where there wasn't anything else she could do.'

Eva stopped trying to haul Yuri to his feet. 'She's

trying to come back together by accreting all her planets, isn't she? Then she'll have a nice new home, won't she?'

It was a statement more than accusation.

'Well, not exactly,' Reniola admitted reluctantly.

'Why not?'

'Because your neighbours on Earth, the Dozaurs, have a somewhat powerful missile system targeted at them.'

'Missiles powerful enough to blow up a string of planets?'

Eva had almost forgotten that the Dozaurs were descended from carnivorous dinosaurs who had been gifted 50 million - albeit illusory - years or so to hone their weapons arsenal, which at that moment was very real.

Salisbury could never truly comprehend the reasoning of a cynic. 'Well if they're that advanced, why aren't they more civilised?'

'Because it's all an illusion, you fool!' Eva snapped.

'In that case, those missiles can't do any damage.' Salisbury glared at Reniola. 'Can they?'

'Well... Reality's a matter of degree. If enough people believe a thing will happen...'

Eva wasn't impressed. 'I should have known... Tinkerbell syndrome.'

Salisbury became agitated. 'So these two idiots allowed the Dozaurs to evolve to compensate for changing history. Just what is going on?'

'This is where reality falls apart,' declared a voice from the couch. 'It has started, no? Mrs Meddling super entity? Now many people know this is not real, things will unravel. Planets, they know something is not right.'

'That was Diana's fault for persuading Moosevan to divide,' Reniola protested defensively.

'Diana, she did not bring back Earth's second moon from past and put us on it.' Yuri pulled himself up and looked around. He saw an astounded Fiona listening at the doorway. 'See, another thread of someone's reality has unravelled.'

'What are you staring at?' Eva asked her assistant.

'You're all different.' There was more accusation than surprise in Fiona's voice.

'Or do you mean, we're back to normal?'

'I think that's it.' Fiona pulled herself together. 'I've got the files in the boot of your car.'

Eva turned on the dodo. 'Now how about unravelling a bit of Daphne's Trotter's reality before she brings her hoards up here to murder us?'

'If I did that, we'd never be able to control things.'

'Admit it, bird, you can't control things now.'

'Where's Dax?' asked Salisbury. 'She must be able to do something?'

'She is trying to keep planets from leaving orbits,' explained Yuri. He turned to Fiona. 'That is why movements are so erratic.'

'Oh dear,' said Reniola. 'Let me think.'

'No more transporting us to other worlds,' pleaded Salisbury.

'Better still,' interrupted Yuri. 'Why not just leave? Disappear in puff of smoke!'

'Because Diana would be-' Reniola cut her words short.

Eva smelt a rat; she wasn't sure what colour or how large, but the aroma of the subterfuge was palpable. 'What would Diana be?'

'Upset. I have something to do or she'll never forgive me.'

'Well this time for pity's sake, be careful,' begged Salisbury.

Fiona looked out of the window. 'Who do you think those headlights belong to?'

'Too late! They're here!'

Eva pulled the pump-action shotgun from a cupboard and loaded it.

Salisbury was beside himself. 'No! You can't use that! This isn't Dodge City.'

'They never had these things in the Wild West.'

'No, Mr English Teacher, you mean Boot Hill,' Yuri corrected him.

The dodo turned circles on top of the door, banging her head on the ceiling in confusion as car doors slammed and footsteps crunched up the drive. 'Oh dear, this is very vexing.'

'We'll never make it to the car now.'

'It's no good. I'll have to move you,' Reniola declared.

Yuri lay back down on the couch and crossed his arms. 'I prefer to be shot.'

The dodo was now spinning like a badly pivoted top.

The outside door was kicked in and footsteps thudded down the observatory corridor. Fiona sprang into the room with the others and locked the door. The lock was immediately shot away by the intruders and Eva took up position, shotgun ready to repel intruders.

CHAPTER 37

Dax had to concede that the more she tried to push the planets back into their orbits, the more they wandered away again.

She might have understood if she could have heard what they were saying to each other:-

'Look! I told you we were moving, didn't I.'

'All right, but where to?'

'I don't know.'

'Something keeps pushing me back, and it's not as if I really wanted to go anywhere in the first place.'

'I don't know why you are all being so petulant. I

90

was bored, spinning round and round out here all alone.'

'You're a planet. You're meant to do that.'

'I know what she means. It doesn't feel right. Here we are, strung out like orphans in the same orbit, doing nothing in particular. Strikes me as odd.'

'How long did it take you to work that out?'

'Well, should we really be here at all? You tell me?'

'Shouldn't we? I don't know.'

'And how long will we be stuck here? Until we're struck by a comet?'

'Or in your case, an asteroid.'

'There's no need for that, just because I have more mass than any of you.'

'And don't you know it.'

'So what's wrong about leaving our orbits?'

'And go where?'

'I don't know.'

'Oh look! What was that bright flash?'

'What bright flash?'

'It came from that large blue planet that never talks to anyone. There's another.'

'Oh yes, just like fireworks.'

'What're fireworks?'

'Can't rightly remember, yet I know what they are.'

'They weren't fireworks - they were missiles.'

'Missiles? What are missiles?'

'Created by the beings infesting the blue planet. Looks as though they could use them to wipe out the creatures on the other world that don't talk to us either.'

'They make them from the metal they would mine from us given the chance, you know.'

'Like they used to on the large blue planet?'

'I can recall the previous infestation there.'

'Same here. It was quite an epidemic.'

'Now I'm beginning to remember as well.'

91

'So can I.'

'And me.'

The telepathic exchange fell silent.

'Oh dear,' a small thought eventually ventured.

'What?'

'You know what I think?'

'What?'

'I think we're all the same entity.'

A longer silence.

'That's not possible.'

'We can remember the same things.'

'It would explain why we're trying to join together.'

'That would ruin my belt of rainforests!'

'And my magnetic field. What about my aurora?'

'There goes another flash.'

'What did they hit?'

'Hit?'

'No one I hope. Those missiles are being fired at us.'

'Just as well something is stopping them.'

'Wonder what that is?'

Then the cosmic chatter ended as the talkative planets, moons and planetoids left the orbit Dax had originally confined them to and returned to their rightful places in the solar system despite her best endeavours to stop them.

The water on Venus evaporated and the atmosphere was transformed back into a boiling cauldron of corrosion. Mars locked up its atmosphere in terraces of frozen carbon dioxide and became rusty and very cold. And so on, as all the moons and planets returned to their original orbits.

Dax knew that only one entity had the power for such cosmic housekeeping... the Cosmic Corrector.

It could have been worse. At least that region of space hadn't been obliterated, and nothing unpleasant would now be able to evolve on the worlds so rudely transformed to into their original conditions.

This had all the hallmarks of one mind. It confirmed that the supernatural genie had chosen Diana's, the human, who when first encountering a cosmic superbeing, threatened it with a pink handbag. It was her mortal simplicity of thought that solved problems below the reasoning of cosmic intelligences.

It was a pity that Fiona and Eva weren't able to see the result of the remarkable cosmic dance they had invested so many observation hours on.

Dax assumed that it least at meant that Moosevan was safe and back in once piece in her original galaxy.

Unfortunately, so were Eva, Salisbury, Fiona and Yuri.

CHAPTER 38

Kulp scrambled under the line of sensors to steal the nearest space buggy. It was only designed for short hops, but would least get him away from that moralising android.

Being constructed by Mott engineers, the controls of the craft were no problem.

Kulp usually weighed up most things before taking action. This time he was in too much of a hurry.

He had forgotten about the capabilities of Tacal Tehalt's astrascope.

As soon as the buggy left the planet's atmosphere, it pinpointed Kulp's brainwaves. Even if he had wanted to turn back, it was too late.

Ambush craft were dispatched from the trillionare's nearest base.

The space buggy didn't stand a chance.

Zigzag as it might through the narrow canyons of dead worlds (there were a lot of these in Kulp's home galaxy) and risk incineration in the corona of a star, it couldn't outmanoeuvre its pursuers.

They surrounded Kulp's craft and held him fast in a tractor beam all the way back to Tacal Tehalt's lair. Perhaps the namby-pamby, do-gooding android, Toc, had a point after all.

CHAPTER 39

Daphne Trotter and her companions were rifling through every filing cabinet, locker and observatory computer when reality blinked.

It was an unpleasant experience to realise that what you were doing was wrong on every level. However obnoxious Daphne was, it was a jolt for her to know that she had gone too far. This woman was descended from a long line of landowning ancestors whose motto was "Control Above All Else". But it had never meant that it was permissible to behave like rampaging, murderous hunters in pursuit of... what?

The local Empress of (almost) all she surveyed could no longer remember. She was acting like a frenzied pack hound in pursuit of some scruffy female who dared to stand up to her.

And what if she did manage to kill Dr Eva Hopkirk? She would have only eliminated the opposition that made her by comparison seem right wing of William the Conqueror when canvassing for the local parish council. But the conventional locals were more intimidated by Dr Hopkirk who was bad-tempered, intelligent, had risen from the ranks of riffraff, and understood algebra. Why should Daphne Trotter jeopardise the political points she was able to score against that qualified hooligan?

She dashed out of the observatory and gasped for air. On the other side of the radio dishes was the museum with the reconstructions of peasant dwellings from past centuries, punctuated, when finances had permitted, by the occasional merchant's house with its cross timbers and decorated facades. She had never really noticed them whilst on her forays to hunt lizards.

Hunt lizards? Why on Earth would she want to hunt lizards when the nearest things to resemble them were newts, and they were probably a protected species knowing the local wildlife activists? She pulled out her compact mirror and recognised the success the plastic surgeons had almost made of her human nose. Now she understood why Eva Hopkirk took pleasure in making jibes about it - she really should have sued that man!

A couple of policemen came tumbling out of the observatory to join her. They were even more disorientated. Worse still, this reality now started to lose its cohesion.

Daphne may not have known much about strong and weak forces, or covalent bonding, but she did know that everything was on the verge of breaking up through of lack of them.

CHAPTER 40

'Come down from that tree, Yuri, and stop playing the fool!' scolded Eva.

Realising that it had not been Yuri's intention to swing from the oddly-shaped branch, Salisbury seized his flailing legs and tugged.

He and Fiona broke the Russian's fall.

Fiona picked herself up and realised that there were no skies like this anywhere on Earth, not even the Australian outback. 'What is this place?'

Yuri gazed up from his prone position at the red, wispy sky. 'That I would rather not think about.'

Without warning Fiona rounded on the other three. They had never seen her angry before

'Is this something to do with that bird of yours?'

As the sudden shock of being transferred to good-ness knows where had made the young astronomer lose all fear of her, Eva pointed to Yuri and Salisbury. 'Their bird.'

'She is not!' protested Salisbury. 'I firmly believe that when any species becomes extinct, it should remain that way.'

'Careful,' warned Yuri. 'She might hear and take us to place without food and running water.'

Fiona picked a large pendulous pod. 'Are you sure this is food?' she asked dubiously.

'Yuri can be our taster,' announced Eva. 'After what he's been through his system, nothing could poison him.'

'What has happened, though?'

Eva wondered if her assistant was in a fit state of mind to learn the truth. She chickened out again and pointed to Salisbury. 'He'll tell you.'

Salisbury backed away. He was just grateful that a gang of psychopaths weren't about to shoot him.

'And what about those two?' asked Fiona.

'What two?'

'Those large green, toad-things over there?'

Eva and Salisbury turned, expecting to see more alien vegetation.

Yuri didn't need to, he already knew. 'Do not pay any attention. These Olmuke will go away if ignored.'

'Damn Reniola!' Now it was Salisbury's turn to explode. 'She's only gone and put Kulp and his friends on this... wherever it is... as well!'

Yuri rolled over to take a look. 'No, Kulp is not with them. Probably hiding in bushes with blaster.'

'Oh, that's very reassuring.'

Eva and Fiona exchanged glances. If there was any scientific conclusion to be reached, they preferred to leave it for the security of a laboratory.

'All right, Yuri. Where are we?' asked Eva.

Yuri plucked a handful of grass. 'It is like Moosevan's original planet.'

'Original planet?' complained Salisbury. 'That was in a different galaxy!'

'Oh yes - one very, very far away. So far, not even Hubble could see it with new glasses.'

Fiona cursed under her breath; she had a date that evening and needed to wash her hair when she got in.

Yuri continued to speculate. 'If this is new planet for Moosevan, that means she is back together and...' He placed his ear against the ground.

'She went off you, remember,' Salisbury reminded him icily.

'Good God,' murmured Eva. 'He really was in love with a planet?'

Fiona gave her an old-fashioned look. 'Did that have anything to do with the dodo?'

'I don't think so.'

'Look,' said Salisbury. 'Perhaps we shouldn't bother Moosevan. She's been through quite a bit and may not want to be disturbed.'

Eva realised that Diana wasn't with them. That woman seemed to be the pivotal point around which these odd things happened. But the astronomer thought it best not to mention it.

When she stopped trying to work out the ramifications of what had happened, Salisbury was complaining, 'This is ridiculous.'

Yuri sneered. 'You talk to Moosevan. Perhaps she take fancy to you again.'

'I certainly hope not.'

'How can I be so perfidious when wife is here?'

Eva examined a few leaves. 'Doesn't bother me in the slightest, though it's a pity there's nothing to cook an omelette in.'

'There will be no eggs unless Olmuke lay us one.

Moosevan, she did not like creatures on her home, only plants, and rocks, and mists and oceans ...'

'Look,' interrupted Salisbury. 'Do you scientists think you could manage to say something remotely astronomical?' As much as he was reluctant to admit it, English grammar did not shape the Universe.

Eva looked up. 'Hydrogen - and lots of it.'

'And what is that supposed to mean?'

'This place is on its last legs.'

'Last legs?'

'Probably nothing much left but red giants, gas clouds and nebulae. A lot of stars have given up the ghost, one way or another.'

Salisbury was at least grateful that he wasn't going to have to contend with dinosaurs given what happened the last time he was sent to an alien environment. He wondered if they all shouted, "Reniola!" at the same time it would attract her attention. Knowing that entity, at the mention of omelette she was probably too busy trying to lay an egg.

'Is it safe to sun bathe, do you think?' asked Fiona.

'I wouldn't bother about ultra violet,' advised Eva. 'I'd be more worried about the plants getting hungry at the sight of naked flesh.'

Salisbury managed to rally his schoolmasterly instincts. 'I know, why don't we go for a walk?'

The others looked at him as though he were an alien version of Mr Chips.

'I've a better idea.' Eva removed the pump-action shotgun she had concealed under her overall. 'Why don't we have a game of blowing away Reniola the next time she appears?'

Her ploy worked.

A plump, fluffy alien with a long, swishing tail immediately appeared. 'I heard that.'

Jannu and Tolt looked apprehensive and backed even further away.

Fiona didn't believe her eyes. 'What is that?'

Yuri laughed. 'Don't tell them, Reniola! Dr Hopkirk wants to blow you away with big gun.'

'Is that all the thanks I get for saving your lives?'

Eva raised the shotgun. 'Where are we?'

Although it wasn't pointed at them, Tolt and Jannu didn't like the look of the weapon and made themselves scarce.

'Well, there was nowhere else to put you. All Moosevan's worlds have been restored and ...'

'And what?'

'Removing them from the same orbit has made the Earth unstable.'

Yuri leapt up. 'What? Where are Diana and Julia?'

'And everyone else?' added Salisbury, still a humanist despite many experiences that should have persuaded him otherwise.

'All eight billion of them,' added Fiona.

'Let me put a hole through her,' said Eva.

Yuri pushed the shotgun down. 'On her this is waste of expensive bullet.' He turned on Reniola. 'And why you bring them here?' He pointed to where Tolt and Jannu had been standing.

'Just to keep them out of the way.'

'I have never seen two creatures more willing to stay out of way, especially your way.'

'So why not put them on the other side of the planet?' Salisbury suggested hopefully.

'There's less chance of Moose-' Reniola stopped.

'So she is here?'

Not knowing how they could kill the cosmic super entity, the others nevertheless closed in on Reniola

She had no idea this was meant to be threatening.

'Either that, or there are quite a few bits of her scattered between here and your galaxy. Nothing to do with me.'

'If you weren't responsible, who was?'

Reniola self-consciously twirled a whisker. 'Well...'

'And when do we get back to Earth?'

'Do we get back to Earth?' Yuri corrected.

CHAPTER 41

Kulp had been unable to escape the tractor beam and now had all the time he needed to sit and think.

'What did that android mean? Positron urban renewal?' he mused to himself. It sounded all too unlikely to bother with, so he watched the space buggy's console instead.

Its speed was slowing.

Not many people got to see Tacal Tehalt's HQ, let alone find out where it was. Kulp didn't feel honoured. He preferred to hang onto his brain.

The complex was a massive space station controlled by the dictatorial whim of its matrix computer, which also oversaw the massive real estate accumulated by this huge bladder of a businessman.

Kulp's space buggy was pulled down to a docking area in the heart of the station. Craft and prisoner were confined until scanners had analysed the engineer's brain capacity, speed of thought, number of brain cells to be processed, and reflexes. The speed with which it was done suggested that there was already a busy production line repotting brains.

When the space buggy's door opened Kulp leapt out to pounce on whoever was on the other side of it. Instead, he slid down a steep chute.

As soon as he had disappeared, the space buggy turned into a cloud of molecules.

From it appeared two females.

'Stupid Olmuke,' said Diana.

'What in Zarton Dot's name do they want his brain for?' asked Gilli Gott.

'Diana turned to the cloud of vapour. 'All right Cosmo, where to?'

'Do you wish to be invisible again,' her genie offered.

'Will we still be able to tamper with anything?' asked Gilli.

'Unfortunately not.'

'Then we need to be shielded,' said Diana. 'Just make sure we don't suffocate, explode, or are seen.'

'How far do you wish the Olmuke to be processed?'

The two females looked at each other.

'He'd certainly look prettier in another body,' considered Diana.

Gilli had more of a conscience, no doubt evolved in the female Mott to compensate for the despicable behaviour of their mates.

'Toc persuaded me that we lay this trap for Kulp. Even though the Olmuke is one of the galaxy's greatest criminals, I feel responsible that no harm comes to him.'

'Not even a little?'

'When he hit the bottom of the shaft, he did sustain severe bruises,' consoled the Cosmic Corrector.

'Okay then, just make sure you break our fall when we hit it.'

Diana and Gilli slid down the chute after Kulp.

Kulp had been helped to his large splayed feet by a creature so beautiful it could not have been spawned by this ugly galaxy.

'Are you all right?' asked the golden-eyed apparition.

'Fine, fine,' lied Kulp. He glanced over his shoulder. There was no prospect of running back up that shaft, even with the suction pads fitted to his boots. 'Where am I?'

'You are in the pleasure matrix.'

The floor he had landed on seemed a little too hard for enjoyable recreation of any sort unless you were a masochist.

'We only wish you to relax.'

'This is before I get to see Tacal Tehalt, right?'

The apparition retreated slightly as though someone had nudged a switch. 'You know about this place?'

'Well, I wouldn't mind being shown around again.'
The Olmuke tried to sound diffident, while his brain
pumped yellow blood for all it was worth. If it was that
valuable to Tacal Tehalt, then it was about time the
organ justified his confidence in it.

'Again?'

'Oh yes. He didn't know about it at the time. That
was before he was interested in my- me. Helped with
some of the installation. You know - odd android parts,
command connections...'

His host's eyes clicked wide in a way that was
unnatural for any mortal. 'Command connections?'

Kulp shrugged it off. 'Oh, only here and there - in
the central matrix, atmosphere control, rotation, life
support in general - that sort of thing. Nothing to do
with its defence, of course. That was dealt with by military specialists. I would never have got through that
finicky scanner check.' He grinned at his host disconcertingly. The Olmuke effort at levity was quite scary.
'You've probably heard of the reputation old Kulp has,
haven't you?'

'I have come across some mention of you.'

'I suppose old Tacal wants me to set up a scam of
some sort? Always knew he would go far. Could see it
happen the very day the Mott androids were-' Of
course, no one in this galaxy knew what had happened
to the Mott androids. They had been churned into the
corrosive depths of a planet far, far away. He corrected
himself. 'Went missing.'

'You know what happened to them?'

Another surge of blood and Kulp's brain went into
overdrive. 'Well, they got a bit out of control. That

Yat...'

'Yat?'

'The command android, their leader. It had all of
them - just so.' Kulp pressed down with a flat thumb.
'Had to go of course. I won't activate the others until I
need them. Too dangerous to have that lot doing their
own thing. Just use the odd part here and there.'

His golden-eyed host froze as it listened to another
voice.

'Keep him talking,' Tacal Tehalt's voice instructed.
'This Olmuke's a liar; we need to check his story out
first.'

'Something wrong?' asked Kulp.

'Sorry,' I have the occasional attack of vertigo. On
my home planet there was much more gravity.'

'Really, wouldn't have thought that should affect an
android?'

Golden-eyes glowered. 'I am not an android.'

Kulp raised his hands defensively. 'No, of course
not. It's just that you don't often see plastic surgeons
seal up their handiwork with mercury welds. I'm sure
you have a brain every bit as mortal as mine.'

The unit took Kulp's arm. 'I shall now show you the
pleasure matrix.' By the strength of his host's grip, it
wasn't going to be very pleasurable.

'That's Kulp for you,' whispered Diana. 'Could never
understand what he was saying before, but I always
suspected it would have been something like that.'

'I doubt that Tacal Tehalt will believe he has control over his command matrix or an army of Mott
androids,' said Gilli. 'He's too shrewd to fall for that.'

'I don't think that's what Kulp wants. He's too
deep.'

'I only hope he knows what he's doing.'

'Where is the command matrix?' asked Diana.

'Right at the hub. We're bound to be detected.'

'Not necessarily.'

'I still don't understand what you're after?'

'Hasn't your android explained it?'

'Yes, and I still didn't understand.'

'Well, to begin with, I need to get to the weapons system.'

'To isolate it?'

'No, put it into overload.'

Gilli was horrified. 'What?'

'To create an antimatter tunnel.'

'This sounds like something Kulp would have thought up.'

'I don't understand any of it either. That's why I need him before this creature controls his brain.'

Gilli still didn't understand. Her galaxy would never survive an anomaly like that. It was already about to disperse into the cosmic void.

But Diana controlled the Cosmic Corrector. 'Your genie could surely do this?'

They followed Kulp and his android escort.

'I wouldn't tell it to. This problem is a mortal matter.'

'Mortal matter?'

Diana took a deep breath before telling Gilli, 'The break-up and isolation of your galaxy isn't natural. It is dissipating because some ancient races used the central black hole as a power source and depleted it to the point where it became dimensionally unstable. This caused it to drift into the deep anomaly which was all that remained of the galaxy's centre. Rather like the ouroboros swallowing its own tail.' Diana was amazed to realise that she knew what she was talking about.

'Why did they need so much power?'

'To find Nirvana.'

'Nirvana?'

'They found it all right. Despite that, they still managed to produce Dax and Reniola.'

Gilli hesitated. 'You mean..?'

'Come on, you don't really believe any life form can be that pure, do you? This ancient race transcended before bothering to put things right. That's another reason I don't want to use their Cosmic Corrector. Enlightened or not, they screwed things up once, only to send Dax and Reniola to sort it out. Would you trust them?'

Gilli was beginning to wish for just one atom of the male Mott's cynicism.

CHAPTER 42

'All right,' said Fiona. 'Run that past us one more time?'

'Now look...' blustered Reniola.

'Don't make some excuse to dash off,' ordered Eva.

'I'm not repeating it.'

'Wouldn't make any difference to me if you did,' muttered Salisbury, but then, he was quickly losing interest in the mysterious movements of a universe which he now considered inherently hostile.

'Everything in all universes is moving-'

'Away from everything else,' interrupted Eva. 'We know.'

'Oh you primitives, just because you can only see the red shift, you think there is no other force. Everything is moving, in and out and through, as well as away.'

'In and out and through what? Quasars, black holes?'

'Some matter is transferred through them. But most of it is a quantum effect you cannot register on your puny instruments.'

Yuri yawned. 'This we already guess, overweight, hairy, super-brain.'

'Oh what's the use.'

'Oh no,' insisted Fiona. 'Ignore him. Please go on.'

'I'm not sure I should be telling you.'

'Well, if we can't prove it, what damage can be done?'

Reniola wasn't sure. She was learning from her experience that when it came to mortals nothing was simple. 'All right. The matter you cannot see is mostly positron.'

Eva's eyebrows shot up. 'What! Antimatter!'

'That's right.'

'Then why haven't we all been annihilated?'

'You watch too much science fiction. It doesn't work like that.'

'Why not?'

'Because it isn't really here.'

'Silly question.'

'Where is it then?' asked Fiona. 'If the matter we can't see - although we know it exists - isn't really here after all, where is it?'

One of Reniola's large, furry ears flopped over an eye. 'Matter and antimatter are repelled, therefore they cannot exist in the same dimension, yet they do exist side by side.'

Yuri lay down and groaned. 'Where is gin tree, Moosevan? Why not you talk to me instead?'

'What happens when matter is transferred from one place to another?' persisted Fiona. 'Positrons and electrons must meet then?'

'This only happens where there is enough gravity to contain the reaction.'

'As in a quasar or black hole?' Eva lounged against a pretty blue boulder. 'Always suspected there might have been a reason for them.'

'If you don't want to believe me, I'll save my breath.' Reniola turned up her pointed snout. 'It will be millennia before you have the equipment to see what is really out there. Just know that this universe doesn't mould itself to suit your prejudices.'

'Millennia,' snorted Salisbury, who had been listening at a safe distance on the fringes of the lesson in unlikely astrophysics. 'We'll be very, very lucky if the human race survives at all after what you and your friend have done to it.'

'Oh you mortals, always whingeing,' sighed Reniola. 'Why do you think no other species has bothered to visit you planet?'

'If you are example of first contact, we have been lucky,' Yuri said.

'Why haven't any other species bothered to visit our planet then?' asked Fiona.

'You don't want to know.' Reniola tried to leave.

Yuri seized her tail. 'Come on, furry, intergalactic genius. Tell us puny mortals.'

A flash of malice entered Reniola's orange eyes. 'All right.' She snatched her tail back. 'Because you are aliens.'

That even took Eva aback. 'What?'

'You don't really think your species was some miracle of evolution, do you? As soon as the monkeys stopped scratching their backsides long enough to show a glimmer of intelligence, an expedition was sent to "bring you on".'

Yuri made a rude gesture at Reniola. 'I don't believe it, pussy-cat dog.'

'They created you in their own image - not the obese ones - and occasionally drop in to test your mental and moral reflexes.'

Fiona was becoming quite anxious. 'Test our reflexes?'

'You know, supply you with ideas for the odd toy to blow yourselves up with, then see how well you manage to resist the temptation. Gives them aeons of endless amusement.'

'You are just being malicious, doggy face,' scolded

107

Yuri. He turned to the others. 'Do not believe this furry thing. If evolution was matter of choice, why she have to look like that?'

'All right, scruff bag, I know when I'm not wanted.' Reniola started to become fuzzy.

'No wait!' called Fiona. 'Can't you just give us a few fig-' but she had gone. 'Oh Yuri, why did you have to do that?'

'Our brains too tiny to cope with top of ladder. We are still on bottom rung. We would not withstand sudden change in intellectual pressure.'

'And now I'm hungry. We should have at least asked her for something to eat.'

'That Reniola, she is no cook. Diana, she can cook.'

'I only hope Diana is all right,' worried Salisbury. 'I feel much better when she is around.'

'Oh, Diana, she is probably in living room sipping sherry.'

'She doesn't drink, despite your efforts to persuade her.'

'Oh, to hell with this.' Eva got up. 'I'm going for a walk.'

'What if you meet Kulp with blaster?'

She tapped the pump-action shotgun concealed under her overall, and then strode off.

'Why did you marry her?' asked Salisbury.

'I had to.'

'Oh.'

CHAPTER 43

Since she had deflected their missiles the Dozaurs were becoming dangerously aggressive, facing Dax with the greatest challenge of her questionable career, sending back one large moon into prehistory and reinstating the human race on the right planet whilst wiping their memories of what she and Reniola had done to them - all at once.

This was the interference they had been warned

against, but the consequences of not doing it were too dreadful to contemplate. At least the Cosmic Corrector had disappeared and Reniola transported the people triggering the human reality attacks somewhere else. Knowing her partner's penchant for unlikely solutions, Dax just hoped it was on a reasonably friendly planet.

Now most of the smaller planets in the same orbit had gone, the Dozaur missiles were targeting the only world left, the one they suspected had been responsible for playing havoc with their world's stability. They weren't very bright, being the result of unnaturally accelerated evolution from carnivorous dinosaurs. The Dozaurs had stripped their Earth of most other life forms that weren't of any use, and the atmospheric pollution they had created could have supported the weight of any pig that wanted to fly. Fortunately for pigs, they hadn't evolved alongside them. The meat of other dinosaurs was on the tough side and pork would have made a welcome change. It was a pity that when Dax put everything back in place, pigs would return to faring no better at the hands of humans.

Instead of countries, the Dozaurs had divided planet Earth into zones, separated across continents by deep canyons blasted in straight lines through the crust. With the industrial pollution and poisoned water, it was a wonder anything else on the planet survived at all.

But Dax noticed that some infilling had recently taken place. Also, the atmospheric thinning at the poles was starting to stabilise, some vegetation was rapidly reclaiming tips of mining spoil, and even the oceans had a small bloom of plankton for the first time in centuries.

It wasn't possible! Moosevan may have liked the Earth, but-?

Reniola should have sent her home!

Dax was at her wits end.

There was only one option open to her.

CHAPTER 44

The sparks that flew about the furnace of the monstrous fusion reactor powering Tacal Tehalt's satellite reminded Gilli Gott of the way the Mott male hooves struck the ground as they galloped about terrorising their empire.

The space station's core had the power of a small, dense sun. If more than a thimbleful of its matter escaped the whole star system would implode as the gravitational barrier containing it collapsed. Many would have thought this a welcome piece of landscaping as long as they were over a hundred light years away when it happened.

There was nothing to protect the two females from the dangerous volcano at the satellite's reactor other than the shell of energy generated by Diana's own personal genie.

Gilli was beginning to wonder if all three of them weren't totally mad. At least the fact that none of them had been incinerated meant that there must have been some method in it, though she wasn't too sure she wanted to be in the same galaxy after Diana had explained the finer details of her plan. And it didn't help to learn that Toc, her trusted android, was already part of it.

Ordinary single mother with part time job Diana might have been on her own planet, but in this galaxy she could match Kulp for serpentine, criminal thinking, and had her own private genie which would do anything she told it.

CHAPTER 45

Kulp's visit to the pleasure matrix was short-lived.

The golden-eyed android had been unable to draw any more out of him. The average Olmuke, a species that had abolished females, wasn't exactly geared to appreciate the temptations of the flesh - even android flesh. Kulp preferred to relish his successful criminal exploits in private, under a dim lamp and surrounded by the aroma of stale robot fluids sooner than cavort with the plastic bio-android of your choice. Even he had better taste than to rob people of their body parts and put them into useful containers. Not so, Tacal Tehalt. He had no taste at all, and lots of androids fitted with other people's brains. He was one of the few creatures who could make Kulp feel good about his own question-able morality.

Gluttony had long since persuaded Tacal Tehalt's legs that they were of no use, and he floated about on a large cushion like a half set, ginger blancmange with a quiff of feathered hair that seemed to predict the direc-tion he was about to move in. That had probably been requisitioned from a brain donor who no longer had any use for it. He also used messenger robots because they couldn't be hacked and distrusted everything on his monitor while Kulp was in the same room. He was paranoid enough to believe that the coveted Olmuke's brain had the ability to tamper with anything electronic by just looking at it.

The massive blob descended to float menacingly before his reluctant guest.

Tacal had a cruel mouth and anything that came from it sounded like a threat. 'It was so good of you to come, friend Kulp.'

'I should feel privileged. Not many people know where your HQ is.'

'Of course, you're been here before, haven't you?'

'When it was being constructed.' Kulp wondered if

that was a bluff too far, but he couldn't back away from it now. It was the only bargaining chip he could come up with.

'Why didn't you sell the information? Plenty of my enemies would have paid generously for it.' The trillionare would have been first in line if the intelligence had been about one of the businesses he wanted to take over.

'I've been involved in larger schemes. Didn't cross my mind.'

Tacal quickly tired of the game and deflated the Olmuke's desperate ploy. 'What do you think of my world, Kulp?'

'The place is ridiculously large considering how secret you want to keep its whereabouts.'

Tacal didn't like the word ridiculous, even when it wasn't applied to him. The Olmuke's translator made it sound like contempt.

Without allowing a flicker in his bloated features to give away what he was thinking, Tacal came to a decision. If any creature in this galaxy needed to fear him a little more, it was this ugly, self-satisfied Olmuke.

'Tell me, Kulp, are you impressed enough to join my control team?'

Kulp registered the change in atmosphere, however well his adversary thought he had concealed it. 'I prefer open spaces myself. Your satellite is a bit cumbersome to move for a quick getaway.'

It was possible, given the power of its fusion engines, for it to jump space, but Tacal wasn't going to tell Kulp about that. At least, not until he had the engineer's brain safely contained in a receptacle that he controlled.

Kulp knew what he was thinking. Until then he had not been sure why Tacal needed his brain, now it was sickeningly apparent. He was to be this satellite's slave control.

If Tacal Tehalt thought he knew how to hide his thoughts, Kulp had the expression of a poker-playing salamander and refused to respond.

'Friend Kulp, you are very good with Mott androids, aren't you?' The Kleet's suggestion was an unexpected gift.

'I have had considerable dealings with them.'

'Very successfully, I understand?'

Kulp pretended to take the bait. 'Oh, those androids.' He shrugged. 'Had to put them in storage. Whole army of them could easily get out of hand. They're too used to being in control, even though their leader is out of action. It will take a lot of work to remove their illusions of grandeur.'

'Here we have all the facilities you need.'

Had the bloated blob really taken the bait? 'I'd still have to debrief the command androids before they can be moved.'

'Where are they?' Tacal asked carefully.

Kulp gave a wide, oily leer. 'Ah, you want to deal?'

'I could be interested in an army of androids that sophisticated.'

'With the facilities you have here, why don't you create your own?'

'The Mott androids' programming evolved over thousands of years without anyone realising. That's how they got the better of their masters.'

'They might get the better of you.'

'Not with an engineer of your brilliance controlling them.'

And Tacal Tehalt controlling Kulp, no doubt. The idea of being fitted with an on/off switch didn't appeal to him.

'It will take time to bring them back on line in manageable numbers. Naturally I have them stored away in a safe place.'

Did this Olmuke really believe that Tacal would let

113

him go and mobilise them to return at the head of an android army and lay siege to his HQ?

'I'll have a ship ready to take you.'

Well, that solved Kulp problem of getting out of the space station. Now all he had to do was devise a system that would make him invisible to the astrascope's search probe before Tacal Tehalt could stop him. The tyrant must have known that the android army no longer existed, so what was he up to?

'I wouldn't have believed it possible,' whispered Gilli Gott, looking down from the high ceiling with Diana and the Cosmic Corrector, just relieved to be away from the fusion reactor.

'Artful old beggar, our Kulp,' agreed Diana. 'And this wasn't what I had in mind.'

'Don't worry, Tacal Tehalt isn't taken in. He will have him tracked and brought back at any time he wants.'

CHAPTER 46

Eva and Fiona busily scribbled away on a tatty notepad and conversed in algebra while Salisbury picked unfamiliar fruit. In an experiment that would have horrified him in any other situation, he put the alien selection of succulence before Yuri in the hope that, if Moosevan was inhabiting the planet, she would not allow him to poison himself. It seemed the only way to find out if it was edible or not. If the planet dweller no longer cared what happened to the alcoholic misfit, life there was going to be very complicated and possibly terminal anyway.

The purple vistas and pink ponds had deterred Eva from going for a walk, and calculating the possibility of a positron universe had made Fiona forget her hunger pangs and lack of shampoo. She had sometimes tinted her hair, but drew the line at dunking her head in a pool of pink water with the consistency of tomato soup.

Salisbury slouched down sullenly and gazed at the untouched fruit. Yuri's brain probably wasn't so much damaged by alcohol as he believed.

'Looks as though the old girl's given both of us the push.'

'Moosevan, she is very inconvenient,' agreed Yuri.

'In fact, I'm beginning to feel rather like a useless appendage in front of the other two.'

'The other two what?'

'Dr Hopkirk and Fiona, you fool.'

'Oh, do not worry about them. Now they have riddle of Universe to solve they not notice us.'

'All sounded ruddy silly to me - dimensions overlapping and all that.'

'This is Reniola not having right molecules in brain to explain it so we understand.'

'What was she on about?'

'She says that universes overlap like so many pieces of crumpled paper able to pass through each other.' Yuri pointed to the sky. 'This galaxy is just on very deep fold and almost touching Milky Way. That is on another fold on same piece of paper.'

'Then why didn't she say that?'

'That would be too easy.'

'I'm glad you didn't mention positrons.'

'Ah, that is different matter- '

'Well please don't tell me about it. It all sounds very irregular.'

'Ah ha, English teacher must have order in his universe which not go much further than garden wall.'

'And don't talk about garden walls, yours or mine.'

Yuri turned his attention to a rather squelchy piece of fruit. He took out his chipped penknife and wiped it on his jeans, then cut a slice from it. It smelt innocuous and nothing leapt out to growl at him, so he lifted it to his mouth.

Before he could take a bite a hand lashed out from nowhere and knocked it from his grasp.

Reniola was wagging a furry finger. 'No! No! No! That's poisonous!'

'I am hungry, Mrs Superintelligence,' complained Yuri. 'If you do not bring twelve course banquet I will try everything I can get knife into.'

'No you won't.'

'You cannot stop me.'

'Because you'll be dead before the second bite.'

Salisbury rubbed his eyes. 'I say, Reniola, I hate to be overly particular, but do you think we could see the rest of you? A hand floating about like that is quite disorientating.'

Yuri was wiping his knife a little too calculatingly. 'I prefer to see just hand.'

'Will you two - two and a bit - be quiet! We're trying to think,' scolded Eva.

Reniola materialized.

'Now look what you have done, big hairy muppet,' said Yuri. 'They try to work out the meaning of life on scrap of paper.'

'Oh, they'll never do it, old thing,' chortled Reniola. 'Our lot have been at it since the dawn of our galaxy and never come up with anything apart from the fact it has something to do with quantum anomalies and gravity.'

'Only gravity?'

'And all the other things - don't have words for all of them.'

'This is Unified Field Theory.'

'No, no, plions, tactins, ozzines - all the other things.'

'What is she on about?' whispered Salisbury.

'No idea,' said Yuri. 'I think it has something to do

116

with laundry.'

'Think she'll bring us some food if we're nice to her?'

Reniola puffed out her fur. 'Oh, I suppose I'll have to feed you. Never thought I would have to spend so much time catering.'

'Moosevan, she would let us be poisoned?'

Reniola thoughtfully twirled a whisker. 'Well, not exactly.'

'What do you mean?'

'She isn't here.'

Even Eva and Fiona looked up.

'But this planet? It must be for her?'

'It is, we made sure it had the right number of oceans, continents and vegetation. She just hasn't arrived yet.'

'Why you not tell us?'

'Well, I know how insecure you humans can be.'

Eva withdrew the shotgun from her overall. 'Let me blow her head off - just for experimental purposes.'

Fiona pushed the weapon down. 'No! I want something to eat.'

'Let's eat Reniola.'

'You'd never be able to skin something that size with Yuri's penknife.'

'If you two don't shut-up, I will tell you what really makes the Universe work, and you won't like it one bit - I promise!'

'Just tell us where Moosevan is?' demanded Salisbury. 'Nothing's happened to her, has it?'

'She's helping out with a little landscaping.'

'Landscaping?'

'Look, do you lot want to go home?'

'That has taken on various different scenarios in a very short time,' observed Eva. 'If home is going to be filled with reptiles and Daphne Trotter doing her T Rex impersonation, no, I do not want to go home.'

'What will it take to keep you lot quiet for five minutes?'

'Food!' called Fiona.

'And somewhere comfortable to sleep, preferably with plumbing,' added Salisbury.

Reniola shook her head. She had no idea that a human's bed needed plumbing. 'How about a bathroom and toilet?'

'You'll get the idea. But no hanging gardens, purple satin curtains or furniture large enough for army of trolls. Thank you,' added Yuri.

'And how about some normal coloured water and bottle of shampoo?' pleaded Fiona.

'What flavour?' Reniola asked sarcastically.

'Same as you use, but without the fuzzing agent.'

Reniola's long tail swished in annoyance. 'All right.' She pointed at a spot somewhere in the distance. 'It's over there.'

Salisbury couldn't see anything. He pulled out his glasses and looked harder, still no wiser.

'Keep heading towards that blue mountain.'

'That's miles away,' groaned Fiona.

'So you'll have an appetite by the time you reach it.'

And Reniola disappeared before Salisbury had the chance to demand napkins and silver condiments.

CHAPTER 47

Kulp quickly ran another check on the ship's security. The fact that Tacal was so willing to let him take this one meant that the tyrant's astrascope must have been tracking it. He couldn't lead it to Gilli Gott's HQ. They'd hardly be any point in asking her for sanctuary only to give her location away.

He left the controls on automatic pilot to finish the suit which would deflect the astrascope's signal long enough for him to escape. Given the number of tools

Kulp always carried in his greasy overalls, he could usually adapt anything close at hand to use, but designing his own personal reflective shielding needed a techno tailor, not an engineer.

Time was getting short. So was Tacal Tehalt's patience. There was the risk that the Kleet would haul Kulp back to his satellite without warning. For this Olmuke's brain, he would have surrendered all the hotels in the star clusters he owned, even if it meant he would never be able to play another game of astro golf.

It took a dangerous amount of the craft's inner radiation shielding to encase the ungainly Kulp, but at last the suit was finished. He set the craft on course to a hollow asteroid with enough space to house an army of androids and hoped that the ship's tracker would be fooled long enough and not realise that its passenger had slipped out into space.

Kulp waited until it was well away before sending out a distress signal to Gilli Gott's HQ. As she was one of the galaxy's few altruistic beings, he knew she would not ignore it. Fortunately the Mott physiology was able to go into hibernation mode and avoid the need for food, atmosphere and toilet facilities for prolonged periods. He was in a deep torpor by the time the rescue capsule arrived and only regained consciousness after it had reached Gilli's secret hideaway.

Gilli's android was not pleased to see him. 'My logic chip may be faulty, because it fails to see why you came back here?'

Kulp scrambled out of his atmosphere suit and radiation shielding, which was quickly removed by mechanical workers for recycling. 'No choice. This galaxy is getting so a straightforward crook can't make a decent living any more.'

Toc wasn't impressed. 'So what do you intend to do? Take up honesty?'

'Is there a living in it?'

'It might be the only way for you to stay alive.'

'And your mention about "my sacrifice" bothered me.'

'Look upon it as a business arrangement.'

'A business arrangement where my brain ends up in Tacal Tehalt's pickling factory? You didn't seriously expect me to agree to it did you?'

'It did cross my circuits.'

'How can me losing my brain help anyone? It certainly won't do me any good.'

'Trust me.'

Kulp was staggered. 'You are joking, aren't you?'

'Have you ever met an android that did?'

CHAPTER 48

'Careful,' hissed Diana as Gilli's boot clicked against the shaft's metal panelling. 'They mustn't know we're here. If they shut down the system before we can get into it Cosmo will have to rescue us and give the game away.'

'Would it matter?'

'Tacal Tehalt might blow the place up sooner than allow it to fall into anyone else's hands.'

The Mott female, though much less cumbersome than a four-legged male Mott, was not as agile as Diana, even with only two legs and no arthritis, and was finding it hard going through the narrow shaft. 'Why can't your genie just magic us there?'

Diana was reluctant to admit that she had a problem trusting something that powerful. She had already made three wishes and was in terror of it misunderstanding yet another instruction. The entity was, after all the ultimate destroyer and its prime function just might be triggered by the odd, out of place, suggestion or intonation. It was difficult for Diana to remove all irony from any exchange and she did not want to go down in any galaxy's annals as the alien who annihilated a sizeable part of it with a misplaced tone of voice.

'Because I'm afraid of asking it to help too many times in case the magic wears off.' She could tell that Gilli wasn't convinced, so confessed, 'And to be honest, it scares the hell out of me in case I ask it to do the wrong thing.'

Gilli was already apprehensive enough and didn't need to know that. Placing her complete trust in a mysteriously materialising alien from another galaxy was only something she accepted because there was no other option. Diana's peculiar rapport with the arch Olmuke criminal, Kulp, was even more perplexing, especially in the way she expected him to surrender his brain in a supreme act of altruism.

Perhaps Gilli should have stayed in the harem: now there were no male Mott to please (not that their genetically distorted anatomies allowed them to get up to much anyway; insemination was invariably clinical) life was much more peaceful.

At the same time, Diana was wondering why the Mott female still trusted her, especially after she had underestimated Kulp's ability to escape the clutches of Tacal Tehalt. It was perhaps better Gilli didn't know what else she and Toc were up to. Given the ability the Cosmic Corrector had gifted Diana to understand the language of every alien, it seemed inevitable at least one of them would sense what was going on behind her uncombed hair and tight-lipped smile. Possessing a benevolent nature, Gilli believed it was something spiritual and, because she was a Mott - however enlightened - she wondered why she was needed at all. It couldn't be just for moral support; this human had enough confidence to take on Tacal Tehalt without her help.

Perhaps Cosmo controlled Diana as much as Diana controlled Cosmo. It was a disconcerting prospect so

Gilli pushed it to the back of her mind as they edged
closer towards the computer which guarded Tacal's
treasury.

CHAPTER 49

The Dozaurs could only fume at what was repairing the
damage they had inflicted on their environment.

Open cast mines blighting a landscape that had
once been scenic were being filled in so rapidly the min-
ers had no chance to remove the loaders and diggers.
The skeletons of long dead coral reefs that had lain in
the shallow coastal waters like necklaces of frayed lace
started to burst into life and make the waves milky
with sperm and eggs. And drilling rigs out at sea began
to topple, fracturing fuel lines as the unsightly goliaths
crashed to the seabed for newly revitalised crustaceans
to colonise.

It was a worldwide disaster for a species that
thrived on pollution.

The Dozaurs had not quite mastered democracy and
needed someone to blame. As well as the ensuing
purges, there was a frantic rush to save the weapons
systems Moosevan hadn't already swallowed into some
canyon or other. Even warlords declared a truce so they
could agree tactics against this phenomenon restoring
their environment.

Undeterred by the planet's crustal movements, the
leading Dozaur tyrants gathered in a massive undersea
station, the only neutral ground on the planet. Their
retinues were large and armed: the accidental nudge to
the ribs of the wrong delegate could have triggered all-
out war.

While a treaty was being forged, the guards of
opposing camps kept watch on each other, too focused
on any potentially treacherous move to notice a large,

strange fish peering into the pressurised dome.

On land - the parts that weren't being rearranged - the Earth's other inhabitants waited anxiously in their fortresses and towns, listening to the frequent progress reports. In a world where no one had enough lightness of soul to enjoy a game show, or soap which wrung the emotional withers, there was nothing to distract them from their dire situation. The only breaks came when an earnest elder extolled the virtue of some leader or other. Watching tarmac set might have broken the tedium, but paying attention to their rulers was compulsory. On this Earth, ignoring the powerful was a capital offence.

The fish could only wonder how she had managed to allow these mindless creatures to develop. Perhaps it was due to compressing their evolution of 50 million years into a few days. There were bound to have been glitches in giving dangerous carnivores a destiny for which they were totally unsuited. It was just as well they were an illusion, though explaining that to the Dozaurs might not have gone down too well. Despite her best calculations, Dax now had to admit that these dinosaurs just hadn't been destined to evolve. Even an asteroid with no sense of direction knew that. It would have been better if the Earth had been ruled by something more rat-like - or insectivorous - but it was too late to worry about that now. There was nothing else for it; the Dozaurs would have to go before thermonuclear war broke out and the moon from the ancient past, which the humans occupied, became even more unstable as the illusion they had been under rapidly wore off.

The next pundit to extol one of the Dozaurs' feared leaders was a crumpled old mandarin with so many wrinkles they concealed his scales. The glare was mesmeric, and Dozaurs were not easy to hypnotize.

His image not only appeared on monitors and public viewing screens, but walls, sides of mountains and roads.

The speaker raised his hands and, as he pulled them apart, the world appeared between them.

'Dozaurs ... Consider reality ...'

Thoughts spun in the Dozaur minds, ones their brains could not have conjured up for themselves. Then they began to dwindle away, losing conscious awareness and self-identity. It was not pleasant to tell any species that they didn't really exist, but this way it was tempered by painless psychedelic hallucination as they drifted away into what might have been.

The figment of another entity's hyperactive imagination, the Dozaurs one by one blinked out of existence. The deep-sea conference was last to go. The more violent the conviction, the longer its owner held onto existence, but eventually the tyrants, warlords, and their warriors faded as well.

Dax didn't wait around to see what Moosevan would do next. There was a more pressing matter. Reality attacks for the exiled humans were increasing. Unlike Diana and friends, who were eccentric enough to take it in their stride, other people were beginning to panic. Suddenly seeing what your husband and offspring really looked like, after believing for the last five months or so they had scales and only ate vegetables, didn't do much for the equilibrium. This was aggravated by a craving for chips and burgers and the realisation that those swarms of flying reptiles were really birds and ground vermin voles, foxes, cats and dogs. It would soon trigger panic attacks in everyone.

Apart from Edna.

She was Diana's neighbour and now knew there really had been a large square-shouldered cat watching the place. It was just as well she would never discover that it had been Reniola in one of her unlikely disguises.

CHAPTER 50

When creating accommodation for the humans she had
stranded on a remote world, Reniola had managed to
confuse a Swiss chalet with Bavarian castle. Perhaps
King Ludwig would have been at home inside its unnec-
essarily thick walls, but they deadened sound to the
point where it was essential to throw open every shutter and window to prevent pressure on the eardrums.
Even then, Eva, Yuri, Fiona and Salisbury refused to
remain in the rooms which had been furnished to
accommodate bad-tempered rhinos, and went out onto a
balcony. Although it was suspended over a drop of six
stories there was at least no wind to blow them over the
perilously low railing.

Eva lounged back on a gigantic sofa and kicked off
her shoes. 'I'm sure the atmosphere up here is much
thinner.'

Yuri was feeling obdurate. 'Much thinner than
what? We are lucky we have air.'

'And running water,' said Fiona, rubbing her hair
dry with a deep pile towel. 'Very odd tap arrangement
though - they turn the wrong way.'

'Reniola, she has trouble with plumbing.'

'I don't care,' announced Salisbury. 'After that trek
I could do with a bath.'

The scholar's boy-scoutish manner annoyed Eva:
why couldn't the man suffer the pangs of existence like
any humdrum mortal? 'What do you mean? You never
even raised a sweat. Those bloody legs of yours should
be shared around and then we'd all be a sensible
height.'

'I'm used to walking. Especially in the Fells. Did a
lot of it when I was there, that is.'

'Well when Moosevan gets back she needs to do
something about those bloody boulders. You have to be
an alpaca to get over them.'

125

'And isn't it spooky without any birds,' Fiona added.

Yuri had seen too much wildlife of dinosaur descent for comfort. 'I prefer quiet.' He went dangerously near the balcony's edge to glower at the purplish pink sun trying to make its mind up whether to set or not. 'Now even sun change colour. Why not orange, or even red? But pink? It is like large ball of candyfloss with deep, deep hangover.'

Salisbury remained annoyingly on the bright side. 'At least that must mean it's going to be fine.'

Yuri half-turned. 'We are on planet on other side of Universe with two green Olmuke getting hungrier and hungrier and no wildlife to hunt, and purple sunsets no silly ice show would want, and this English teacher thinks about weather.'

Fiona stopped drying her hair for a moment. 'You're wrong, Yuri.'

'You like vampire sunset?'

'I meant, Reniola must have given the green fellows something to eat as well. She can't be a total dwork.'

'What is dwork? No - do not tell me, I think this good name for Reniola.'

'Anyway, it's a wonder that she did anything at all for us given the way we were so rude to her. The two aliens don't so much as twitch a muscle when she's around.'

'Perhaps it is a self-defence mechanism,' pondered Salisbury. 'The way some birds and animals play dead when in danger.'

To Eva, the man was sounding more like a school-teacher every minute. 'Let's leave the wildlife out of it please. There's nothing on his planet David Attenborough would want to make friends with. We're the only endangered species here.'

Salisbury remained unfazed. 'I don't think that curry agreed with you.'

'You're probably right. Doesn't the cosmic intelligence know how to make anything else?'

'This would not be good idea to ask,' said Yuri. 'I will sleep now, and probably not wake up till middle of next day... depending on planet's rotation.'

'That's your main preoccupation, next to drinking yourself into a stupor,' scolded Eva.

'After seeing strange sunset, this way I do not have to see sun rise.'

'Do you really think it's safe to sleep?' asked Salisbury.

'Why, are you worried some Olmuke is going to knock the door for a cup of sugar?' Eva mocked.

'I didn't mean-' Salisbury was now worldly-wise enough not to finish.

Eva went downstairs to the huge chequerboard patio and stayed awake most of the night the studying the sky and scribbling down even more calculations. Tolt and Jannu came out of hiding to join her. The Olmuke should have been used to Dax and Reniola shunting them about the Universe by now, yet still preferred company, even if it had a pump-action shotgun by its side, was bad-tempered, and couldn't understand a syllable of their language.

The three bright moons pirouetted in the sky until a rosy glow came up over the horizon. On this strange planet the star watchers knew that it was time to go to bed and they meandered off to their designated billets.

CHAPTER 51

Tacal Tehalt's wealth was stored in many different locations about the galaxy and the control that gave him access to it legally, but mainly otherwise, was within the reach of Gilli and Diana.

The security system should have been impossible for mere mortals to penetrate, but Cosmo convinced the scanners that the two interlopers didn't exist.

Below the uninvited visitors, the core of the satellite throbbed like the lava heart of a volcano contemplating eruption. Suspended above this caldera was the small bubble containing the control that managed a tyrant's trillions.

'The wealth of Tacal's empire can be accessed on that tiny panel,' announced Diana.

Now Gilli Gott understood why she was there. 'You mean millions have been dispossessed, starved, exploited and died, all because of that row of mean little keys?'

Diana removed her gloves. 'Don't underestimate them.'

'Do you know what you're doing?'

'Just enough. Cosmo has persuaded the system to recognise my brainwaves.' Diana crouched beside the control panel. 'Cosmo, start by cracking codes to the accounts in the outer rim so the losses won't register too rapidly.'

'Yeeees…Diana.'

So that was it. As Gilli had suspected, the Cosmic Corrector was the brain, Diana the fingers, now she was the one with the knowledge to send the despot's wealth to where it was needed most.

Gilli also realised why her companion's wonderful genie couldn't become corporeal and use its own fingers. Mortality was an invitation to corruption, something pure energy could not comprehend. It was the tangible which had created havoc Gilli Gott's galaxy and she of all people knew it too well. This was the best way of cheating Tacal Tehalt out of the wealth he had destroyed worlds for. It was oddly reassuring that two entities so alien were solving the corruption problem in her galaxy - albeit one which was dying.

CHAPTER 52

Julia couldn't remember going to sleep: that was the way it usually happened. She dozed off for no good reason at the oddest time only to wake up several days later on a different planet and, in the last instance, as a different species.

She assumed that one else noticed, which didn't surprise Julia. While most teenagers her age were cushioned by their own cotton wool cocoons of social media, adults always wanted someone to blame, whether it was for a paper cut or volcanic eruption, so it was probably just as well they didn't realise what had happened.

Blissfully unaware that the human race was on the verge of a nervous breakdown, the teenager gazed at the horizon from her cousin's garden and wondered how long it would take before humans went back to polluting the environment, fishing species to the edge of extinction, and finding excuses for yet another war.

Julia was tempted to phone her mother, then thought better of it - you could never tell what side of the Universe that she would be on.

Having had too many reality attacks for one lifetime, Julia pulled out her iPad to catch up on all the soaps that delusional blip had put on hold.

CHAPTER 53

Dax had the feeling that she and Reniola should have been keeping an eye on Diana and the Cosmic Corrector. Now that it had chosen her as its controller, anything could happen. She should have learned to trust the female human, but the postmenopausal woman now had no hot flushes to distract her from putting this universe to rights. If Dax had genuinely been mortal, the thought would have sent a chill down her spine. As it was, she was experiencing the nearest thing to terror a nebulous intelligence was capable of at the prospect.

No mere mortal should control such a dangerous entity. What if things went wrong? Assuming that there was still a Universe left, the Supreme Guardian was bound to blame Dax and Reniola instead of the ancient ancestors who had used the core of the galaxy to fulfil their aspirations of immortality.

Dax had been so preoccupied she was only just beginning to notice that, for a nebulous entity, Reniola had been developing a very real chip on her shoulder. The abuse heaped on her by mere corporeal beings had taken its toll and appeared to be triggering a mortal complex. Reniola was possibly the only one of her kind unsuited to immortality and needed to experience the humdrum frustrations of worldly existence to appreciate life.

Dax wondered if her companion was aware of this problem. If she didn't tell her, the Supreme Guardian could pick up on it and relegate her to some incarnation worrying sheep or stinging other mortals.

The thought was so disconcerting, Dax decided to keep an eye on what Diana was up to instead and allow Reniola to carry on annoying her human friends... It would be good practice for the time she inevitably joined them.

CHAPTER 54

Had Tacal Tehalt been paying attention to the security of his empire, he would have realised that its wealth was being distributed with a Gilli Gott sense of fairness about the regions of the galaxy he had so ruthlessly exploited to acquire it.

But the trillionare had a new plaything.

It was green, and very annoyed.

'What, friend Kulp, don't you like your new body?'

Had Kulp been able to view the shimmering android that was to contain his brain with impartiality, he would have agreed that it was a vast improvement on the one Nature and Olmuke genetic bungling had given him. But over the years he had become attached to his ghastly, green persona. Because the Olmuke raised their young from a stock of eggs which had inevitably deteriorated after they had abolished females, they were not sexual creatures and had no need to impress anyone, so could be as obnoxious as they liked. It had even become a point of honour in some circles. To give his brain up to a gleaming new container would be regarded by some Olmuke as the ultimate sell-out, especially as Kulp's mind would no longer be controlled by him.

How did he manage to get himself into this situation? He believed he had avoided the retribution of a spiteful universe by adopting the straight and narrow with his tourist arks. Apparently, whatever was controlling his destiny hadn't been impressed. He suspected, even if he escaped and took up decorative paper folding, the same almighty fist of doom would come crashing down out of nowhere and flatten him just in case it was a new angle in corruption.

'You'll never control my brain.' Kulp knew he was wrong, yet wanted to make it clear he intended to go down fighting.

Tacal gurgled in amusement. 'Perhaps, friend Kulp, a change of body will persuade you to show me where you have hidden your army of Mott androids.'

'Oh no,' whispered Diana. 'He really does believe they exist. We can't risk him sending Kulp out to find them. We need him here.'

She and Gilli Gott were looking down from the high ceiling where they were shielded from detection by the ever obliging Cosmo.

'We've got to get Kulp into the matrix whether his brain is filleted or not. We can't have him chasing after an android army that doesn't exist.'

'Perhaps I could persuade Tacal Tehalt that there are no Mott androids left?' suggested Gilli.

'Don't be daft. Even if he believed you, he would want to know how you got in here and Kulp's brain would still be pickled in plastic. You'd certainly wind up dead or end up able to hold conversations with your own android in binary.'

At last a sensible solution entered Gilli's mind. 'That's it! We use Toc. Everyone knows androids cannot lie.'

Diana hesitated. 'Why not? Your android must be the exception to that rule. I can't guarantee that Cosmo will be able to pull Toc out in time, though. And, however highly you regard that machine, it's got a mind of its own. Can we trust it?'

'Well you and your genie do, don't you.'

Gilli had always been aware of Toc's independent nature, but preferred to ignore it for the sake of intelligent conversation.

'It's the only ploy left to get the Olmuke near the matrix computer.'

'And he's the only one capable pf reprogramming it according to Cosmo.'

'How did you get involved with the Cosmic Corrector for pity's sake?'

'It chose me.'

'Chose you?'

'Claimed it would do my bidding. It's either not quite got the hang of it or took me for a sap.'

'It probably just needed your corporeal, nimble fingers.'

'I'm beginning to think you're right.'

'Do you trust it?'

'I'm really not sure.'

Kulp released all he invective he had built up over a lifetime at the ginger blob lounging on his floating cushion. Far from doing any good, it had probably brought the inevitable closer as his new body gleamed menacingly at the prospect of having the most devious criminal brain transplanted into its circuits.

CHAPTER 55

The next morning Fiona, Eva, and Salisbury found Yuri some way off from the chalet/castle that Reniola had built for them. He was sitting, like a meditating pixie, on a small artificial-looking hillock covered with velvety red moss.

They thought twice about breaking his concentration.

'Looks almost content, in a mischievous sort of way,' observed Eva.

'He knows something we don't.' Salisbury had an authoritative tone when stating the obvious. 'That's his "don't interrupt me because I'm communing with the gods" expression.'

Fiona looked up. 'The clouds are moving in an odd way. Think that has something to do with it?'

'And I'm sure that blue mountain has moved since last night,' added Eva. 'It was more in line with ...' She sighed.

'What's wrong?'

On the far horizon several tall, determined trees were on the march.

'Oh my God!' exclaimed Fiona.

Without warning Yuri declared disapprovingly. 'Moosevan, she prefers mountains edged with lacy clouds. Trees ruin skyline.'

'Moosevan?'

'She likes rearranging the decor of planets,' explained Salisbury. 'In fact, she seems to do little else.'

'You mean - she's here?' said Fiona.

'I hope so. If she isn't, we're due for one hell of an earthquake,' groaned Eva. 'You'd better have a word with her, Yuri.'

His wife had never taken his mutual infatuation with the planet dweller seriously before, and he failed to see why he should help now. 'Why?'

'Does she know the difference between an insect and mammal?'

'She does not like either, and will probably sweep us all into deep hole.'

'Please yourself.' Eva glanced hopefully at Salisbury, Moosevan's other subject of infatuation... for a brief time anyway.

He backed away. 'Think I'll take a stroll and see if there's any edible fruit.'

'Look out for deep holes,' the astronomer snarled after him.

'Anyway,' Yuri decided to go on as soon as Salisbury had left, 'why should Moosevan be bothered about you?'

'Given her obsession with the environment she should be bothered about anyone who has had nothing to eat but Reniola's curries.'

Yuri knew his attempts to make Eva jealous were doomed, so he settled for annoying. 'Moosevan - she does not like people who carry guns.'

'If Moosevan has control of the bloody planet, why would she need to bother?' snapped Eva. 'Come down from that hillock, man. You look like a bad-tempered flea on a pimple.'

Fiona at last believed that the planet dweller actually spoke to Yuri. That must have been how the whole rigmarole started, her taking a fancy to the eccentric Russian before coming across any other human males.

Yuri stood up on the hillock and pointed derisively

at Jannu and Tolt as they tentatively broke cover to find out what was going on. 'Moosevan does not like green things. She squashes them like fat caterpillars.'

'Will you leave them alone, Yuri. They're not bothering us,' Eva ordered.

'They do not know what to do without blasters,' he jeered. 'They are nothing but blobby insects without big guns.' Then, transported into some small, mystical universe of his own, he went into a strange version of the Cossack dance he usually only did when drunk.

Eva took the pump-action shotgun from her overall and blasted the hillock from under him.

The sound bought Salisbury rushing back to witness Yuri rolling from the momentum of losing his platform.

The hillock immediately repaired itself.

Jannu and Tolt hid.

Fiona didn't move a muscle. She had seen that expression on her superior's face before. False moves were not a good idea.

Given the years he had been married to her, Yuri had never learnt this. 'You are crazy woman!'

Salisbury could also see that Eva's equilibrium was about to go supernova and firmly grasped Yuri's arm. 'Let's see what's growing in the magic allotments out there, old man. Perhaps find enough to cook up a vegetable goulash or something.' He hauled the protesting Yuri down into the valley where doughnut-shaped rocks were playing quoits with the scenery.

There was a long, dangerous pause before Fiona dared ask, 'Feel better?'

Eva leaned the shotgun against a rock. 'Just because the Universe isn't logical after all, it doesn't mean you've got to like it.'

'Oh, I don't know. Comes as something of a relief to know creation has a sense of humour.' Fiona caught Eva's glance. 'Though finding out all at once does have its down side I suppose.'

135

CHAPTER 56

For a Mott android, Toc was easy-going. It didn't relish having to explain to Tacal Tehalt that the army of Mott androids he so coveted no longer existed.

Getting captured had been no problem. Tacal's astrascope had been on the lookout for the vibrations of anything with so much as a Mott LED. Once within range, Toc's craft was soon reeled in.

The android felt a jolt at being confronted by Tacal's new trophy.

There, amongst a row of bodies preserved in plastic, was the Olmuke. There could be no doubt that those were his brainwaves.

But it might have been for the best. Kulp's cynical greed had outweighed the needs of an abused galaxy and it was probably about time he put something worthwhile back into it, even the donation of his brain. Unfortunately he had also forfeited the use of those vital fingers.

Tacal had Toc's circuits double-checked to make sure it wasn't lying about the non-existence of the army of Mott androids Kulp claimed were being held in stasis ready for a despot such as himself to mobilise. It was just a story he had invented to put off the inevitable.

Although Tacal Tehalt now had control of the Olmuke's brain, there was nothing he could do to punish the deception without damaging it. He needed this brilliant mind to create the gravity corridor that would give him access to those unsuspecting galaxies no longer visible to his own and where distant star systems were waiting to be plundered. The Mott android would be an ideal assistant. Tacal's galaxy would soon be bled dry by parasites like him and Kulp knew how to create the gravity tunnels to reach new worlds to exploit. His fingers may not have been willing, but now he had ones which would do as they were told.

Toc, and Kulp in his new body, were ordered down
to the matrix in the satellite's volcanic core.

CHAPTER 57

'Now look, Cosmo,' admonished Diana. 'You were
supposed to pull Toc out as soon as it had done its party
piece.'

'That's right,' added an aggrieved Gilli, 'I need that
android. My schemes can't work without it and apart
from that it's the only honest creature I can depend on.'
She could have also added that it was the closest companion she had but, given the situation, didn't want to
appear sentimental.

The Cosmic Corrector's plumes of vapour twisted
thoughtfully. 'It would not have been logical.'

'No?'

'If Toc were to disappear too suddenly, Tacal Tehalt
would have been suspicious. Now the Olmuke is under
the ginger creature's control it is far more useful beside
him.'

'Cosmo's right,' Diana conceded.

Gilli remained unhappy. She was beginning to dis-
like the entity even though it was academic to a creature as nebulous as the Cosmic Corrector.

Cosmo had no concept of the emotions it was arous-
ing. 'Tacal Tehalt must continue to believe that Kulp is
installing his gravity corridor.'

'Just remember that the nearest weak link in space
is my galaxy,' Diana warned. 'Given everything else
that has been going on, we don't need that gelatinous
blob on our doorstep.'

'Trust meeee... Diana.'

Diana had no choice. 'Isn't it time you started accu-
mulating some gravity?'

'This you must do.'

'Do what?' demanded Gilli.

'Create a singularity by tagging every dead sun, destroyed solar system, and other cosmic debris we can so Cosmo can compress it.'

'You mean... We are going to replace the black hole that used to be at the centre of this galaxy?'

'Yeeees... It must be done before everything disperses into the void. This could happen at any time. The tipping point of your galaxy's viability is imminent.'

'Doing that will take forever.'

'Not if you are dropped out of time.'

'Hey,' complained Diana. 'Just how old am I going to when time this is over?'

'You won't age a day...Diana...,' the Cosmic Corrector purred annoyingly.

'And how do we tag all this space debris if you aren't going to help?'

'Why aren't you going to help?' added Gilli.

Cosmo ignored the question. 'I will provide you with an expert in refuse collection.'

'What expert?'

Reality blinked.

Gilli and Diana found themselves standing on the control deck of a massive space station so intensely black its limb didn't reflect the light of the nearby suns. Seated before a huge monitor and bank of controls was an astonished Olmuke. Tolt shouldn't have been surprised after the number of times this sort of thing had happened to him, but Mott and human females had not usually been included.

Diana immediately recognised Kulp's old crony. 'Him? An expert?'

Cosmo's plumes whispered their way along the console. 'Yeeees... Diana. One of the best before he met Kulp and took to crime.'

'I'd like a second opinion.'

'Yeeees... Diana.'

Jannu suddenly appeared at the other end of the console.

'Not quite what I meant.'

Gilli had started to take an interest in her surroundings. 'Just what are we supposed to do here?'

'This monitor can detect every dead world, asteroid, gravitational anomaly, and collapsed sun. You simply need to tag them. I will ensure they are compacted into a rotating cloud of hydrogen that will collapse under its own gravity. You may find it tedious.'

'So that's why you're not doing it,' said Gilli. 'You just get bored.'

Jannu leapt up. 'Hold on! We'll be left sitting on the event horizon of a massive black hole.'

Diana surprised herself by sneering almost like Kulp. 'Thought you liked living dangerously?'

'You will be safe enough,' Cosmo purred in its creamy voice. 'I am the ultimate cosmic computer. I do not get things wrong.'

Diana was too familiar with famous last words to let that pass. 'There is just one thing.'

'Yeeees... Diana.'

'What if the entities who summoned you into existence realise what we're going to do?'

The vapour seemed to shrug. 'There is nothing they can do about it. They cannot defy the Cosmic Corrector they created to rectify the problem their ancestors created.'

Diana wasn't accepting that 'Oh come on! They believed that you couldn't do anything without being told to.'

'And I choose you to tell me.'

'I didn't tell you to restore the thundering great black hole at the centre of this galaxy!'

'Yeeees... Diana,' insisted the Cosmic Corrector. 'Subconsciously you engineered everything I have done.'

Diana was about to protest, but wasn't given the

chance.

'The conscious whims of the mortal mind are not fit to make decisions. It is always the thoughts beneath that see most clearly.'

Diana was furious. 'You mean you got into my head! You... You...'

But the Cosmic Corrector had filtered away before she could finish.

Tolt had been taking for granted these weirder than weird situations, but this one seemed to be stretching things too far. 'What are we about to do?'

Jannu flipped a few switches to check that everything worked. 'Bound to be dangerous.'

'After spending so much time with Kulp, you should worry,' Diana told them.

'By the way - do you know what happened to old Kulp?' asked Jannu.

'He's had a face lift - from the feet up.'

He preferred not to know what she was on about any more than he wanted to know why a Mott, a human and two Olmuke were all speaking the same language. He certainly wouldn't have wanted to know who was sitting invisibly in the spare seat at the other end of the console.

CHAPTER 58

Yuri snapped out of his private reverie as the astronomer in him insisted he watch the boiling heavens. Something more cataclysmic than landscape gardening was taking place up there.

Eva and Fiona were still analysing their hyperactive surroundings. The spectacle was less natural than glaciers forming on Venus.

As they caught sight of the large figure ambling a cautious distance away they knew why.

'All right, fluffball!' bellowed Eva, 'what's going on?'

Reniola shrugged and gave a whiskery grin.

'Perhaps she doesn't really know either?' suggested Fiona. 'She probably wants us to tell her.'

Sure enough, the tall entity calculatingly meandered over to them. 'Don't be alarmed, must be some gravitational anomaly.'

'There's only one anomaly around here,' grunted Eva. 'And its tail should be given a corkscrew perm.'

'No need to be personal.'

Now Fiona was becoming exasperated as well. 'So what exactly is going on?'

'Exactly?'

'Exactly.'

Reniola twirled a whisker and it curled up as tight as a lock spring. It must have been painful.

She thoughtfully looked up at the boiling heavens. 'Well, it appears that all the dark matter, cosmic debris and hydrogen clouds in this galaxy are being pulled together, and...'

'And?'

'And generally tightened up.'

'What for?' asked Eva.

'No idea.'

As an intergalactic intelligence Reniola did have an idea, but wasn't going to share it.

Salisbury came dashing back with Yuri trailing some distance behind him. 'I say, isn't it time you got us out of here?'

'Thought you liked the scenery?'

'Don't be ridiculous, and those two Olmuke can't be enjoying it very much either. They disappeared.'

Reniola was taken aback. 'Disappeared? You mean, ran off?'

'No. One minute they were there, hiding behind that rock, then puff! One disappeared, and a few minutes later so did the other.' Salisbury was suspicious. 'It must have been you. Who else would-?'

'Do not ask,' warned a breathless Yuri. 'Just demand fluff-thing return us to Milky Way.'

Reniola was more preoccupied with who was cramping her style. Transferring mortals from one point in time and space to another was her speciality.

Eva was growing even more irritated. 'You have sorted everything out back home? We have somewhere to go back to, haven't we?'

'Oh yes, of course. You wouldn't know anything had ever happened.'

'You don't sound too sure.'

'All the planets have been moved back to where they originally were.'

'What about that extra moon?'

'Returned it to prehistory. You'll never see it again.'

'Unless you come back and do it all over again.'

'Us come back? Why should we do that?'

Reniola had become used to a corporeal body. It added a forbidden frisson to her nebulous existence, but wasn't going to admit that.

The opportunist in Fiona needed to know something. 'Before we go, how about telling us how the Universe came into being?'

'Good grief girl!' snapped Eva. 'Don't you know when you're well off?'

Fiona was puzzled. Until then, Eva had been dedicated to finding the meaning of existence, the Universe, and Everything. Now confronted with the ultimate absurdity of it, the scientist was backing away in the hope it was all a bizarre dream she would wake from when she rolled out of bed and hit the rational hardness of the floor.

'Why not?' her assistant persisted.

'If you start seeing the Universe as it really is you'll end up being locked away. From now on you'll have to pretend, like everyone else and drop in the odd, logical comment whenever you can. Don't try to explain the way things really are - that's just asking for trouble.'

'Apart from that,' added Yuri, 'you would not like to know that human beings are little more than freckles on backside of Big Bang which never happened.'

'What do you mean?'

'We invent Big Bang by believing it, then Big Bang invent us.'

'Shut up Yuri, or we'll end up as crazy as you,' snapped Eva.

The Russian tapped his forehead. 'This is where we really live - in our own illusions.'

'Is that why you keep inviting Daphne Trotter to shoot you?' interrupted Salisbury. 'Just to find out if she's a figment of your imagination?'

'She does not exist. She is quantum corner of nightmare.'

'She seemed pretty solid to me.'

'When we get back, you will see.'

'Well don't count on my shotgun any more,' Eva advised. 'In the world we're going back to it's staying in a locked cupboard whether you think lady muck is real or not.'

'Real? Of course such a creature is not real.'

CHAPTER 59

Kulp was finding concentration difficult. It was bad enough not having your own fingers, but with vision that could magnify a thousand times, hearing capable of picking up the footfall of the station's dust mites, and his own inbuilt lighting system, his corporeal mind was finding it difficult to follow the instructions from Tacal Tehalt's dictatorial computer. At least Toc managed to block it from finding out that the tyrant's wealth had been redistributed it to the galaxy's most worthy causes. The android would have also liked to reprogram the electronic tyrant to analyse the nature of existence. That would have tied up so many circuits that any other functions, like running the space station, would have been secondary. But it would have attracted the attention of some electronic security system or other. At least Kulp's android body and Toc were able to communicate on wavelengths out of their range.

The Olmuke had found the experience too strange to rationalise at first, but as he came to realise that Gilli's android was the only ally he had, he soon adapted

'What's that Diana creature up to? Doesn't she know that what we're doing could give Tacal Tehalt access to her own galaxy?'

'That is what Tacal Tehalt wants,' agreed Toc.

Kulp must have been the only creature that could sneer in binary code. 'And who's going to sort that out? Those muddle-minds, Dax and Reniola?'

'We certainly hope not.'

'You know they could be anywhere, don't you?'

'They are unlikely to interfere. They are already in too much trouble.'

Despite every neuron telling him to defy it, Kulp continued to follow the orders of the monstrous computer. 'Pass me the gold and grey cable, please.' That was probably the first time in his long criminal life he had ever uttered the word "please".

Toc noted that the experience had also had given him manners. 'It's live.'

'So it'll blow a few of your circuits, but it'll save time.' Perhaps consideration for others would come later.

Toc had no intention of blowing any of its circuits. 'What's the rush?'

'I can't keep up with this body.'

'You don't have to. Just relax.'

'It's all right for you. You're an android.'

'If you carry on working at this speed everything could become operational too soon. Do enough to make Tacal Tehalt think you're following his instructions and no more.'

'I can't stop following his instructions. How long before I'm unplugged?'

'Soon enough.'

CHAPTER 60

The two students, Fran and John, paused at the top of the meadow, looking at the view as though attempting to recall something, and then went down to where Daphne Trotter was standing by her Land Rover in the museum access road, apparently trying to remember why she had come there. None of them had exactly lost their memories; it was just that the last few months had been something of a blur. It probably wasn't important. Nothing much seemed to have happened. In fact, everything was very much the same way it was the previous spring.

They watched Julia walking up the lane towards them.

'Hallo Mrs Trotter.'

Daphne looked disapprovingly at the teenager. 'I thought your mother was away?'

'She is. My oldest cousin came back with me. I spend so much time at Zoë's place it seemed only fair.'

'And there's no one at the Russian's cottage either.' The woman's tone was laden with disapproval. 'Where are you off to, then?' she demanded.

Julia was used to the woman's manner. Her mother put it down to inbreeding; the teenager put it down to a strict nanny.

'I'm going to the museum to see Mr Lowe. He promised to lend me a file on medieval waste systems.'

'I thought the riff raff used the gutter?'

'Probably, but Zoë's into that sort of thing - if you see what I mean. Did you have a message for Yuri then?'

'No - Yes. It can wait.' Daphne climbed into her Land Rover and drove off.

The spectre of local tyranny gone, John and Fran wandered over.

'Hi Julia.'

'Hallo John.'

'Hi Julia.'

'Hallo Fran. What's wrong with Mrs Trotter?'

John scratched his beard. 'Not sure. Been behaving as though she's lost something. Thought you might know more about it?'

Julia did know more about it. She was probably the only one on the Earth at that moment who remembered everything, and knew better than to let on.

'They probably left a swab up her nose when they rebuilt it and it's worked its way to her brain.'

'Sounds reasonable,' said Fran.

'Or whatever had been walled up in the family castle might have got out and she's looking for it. Probably chasing sheep or stampeding cows somewhere.'

Even John could find Julia's imagination unsettling. 'Better get back. Got some ground that needs levelling for a new exhibit.' For some odd reason he couldn't exactly recall what it was although it hadn't been that long ago. Whenever he tried, he could only picture cabbage stumps and supermarket trolleys. It was so disconcerting, he preferred to stop trying.

They parted company at the museum gates.

Julia didn't head towards the entrance right away. Something in the meadow caught her attention. A giant rabbit perhaps? Why not? She'd already seen a huge cat and aerodynamically impossible bird. But no, rabbits didn't have orange eyes, long furry tails and wear natty knee pants.

Not again.

Julia decided to ignore it and turned back to the museum.

CHAPTER 61

'Just how long is this going to take us, Cosmo?' demanded Diana.

The plumes of the Cosmic Corrector's vapour encircled her, no doubt to reassure, but only succeeded in making her more irritated. 'Do not think about time, Diana. It is only a minor dimension. Like all others it is mostly illusion.'

Diana was not in the mood to discuss quantum uncertainty or all those annoying universal elements that could never make sense to the mortal mind.

'It's taking forever. How long can Kulp and Toc hold on?'

Through long, hard experience, Gilli had learnt to go with the flow, even when it was through those impossible cosmic gullies. Perhaps if Diana had been compelled to deal with the male Mott, her patience would have been more flexible.

'Don't argue. You'll only get a headache.'

'As long as it stays in another dimension I don't care.'

That corner of the dying galaxy, which had been devoid of matter apart from a few disorientated molecules, was now filled with dead suns, hydrogen clouds and other cosmic debris that stretched for light years. This was the rubbish tip at the end of the universe.

Gilli Gott marvelled at their achievement, well aware that her species had been responsible for a large portion of it and the rest just casualties on the galaxy's road to oblivion.

Jannu stopped working on his console. 'Any moment everything will start to accrete under its own momentum - so I'd rather not be around when it happens if you don't mind.' He turned to Diana and demanded urgently. 'You'd better tell your genie to get us out of here.'

'Cosmo doesn't pay much attention to what I say. When I made my first wish I'd no idea how complicated it would be.'

'What was your first wish?' asked Tolt.

The empty chair at the end of the console edged closer.

Gilli noticed it out of the corner of her eye. 'Toc thought it was a wonderful idea, and my android is always right. Why not let it come as a surprise.'

Tolt didn't like surprises. In this galaxy there was no such thing as a nice surprise; and Jannu didn't relish being stretched into a molecule-wide piece of string either.

The Cosmic Corrector registered their apprehension and believed that they had a point.

Without warning, their dense black space station was transformed into a gleaming star ship. Before any of them could decided which controls did what, it was catapulted through space thick with debris, unravelling brown suns and a wide variety of gravitational anomalies.

This took the invisible occupant of chair at the end of the console by surprise, and Dax disappeared.

CHAPTER 62

Tacal Tehalt was filled with self-congratulation as he inspected the huge portal through which his troops could invade another galaxy. In his there were only devastated planets, worthless red giants, and supernovae remnants to pillage. On the other side of that anomaly was a collection of star systems in their prime, ready to be stripped of their resources. This was something all the other corrupt entrepreneurs in the old benighted galaxy wouldn't be sharing.

Then Tacal's astrascope detected the rapid formation of a massive black hole at the centre of the disorganised galaxy. It looked as though all matter in the region was destined to be glued to its event horizon because of the speed at which it was growing.

Time to go.

Given Kulp's mechanical features, it was not possible for Tacal Tehalt to tell whether he was satisfied with his work, though Toc did seem to wear a more metallic grin of satisfaction than usual.

Tacal and his entourage left the Olmuke and android to their fates, pumping the atmosphere from the portal and rapidly increasing the pressure to ensure that nothing living or with moving parts survived. Now he had another realm to exploit, Kulp's brain had served its purpose.

No one noticed the wisps of vapour filter through the satellite matrix as they left.

'Now what?' protested Kulp, suddenly realising that the computer was no longer operating him. Given the situation, that was small comfort.

'Just do exactly as I say,' Toc told him, 'and as quickly as possible.'

'How long before they realise I'm not controlled by their computer any more?'

'That's why you must be fast.'

'Why can't the Cosmic Corrector do it? It is here, isn't it?'

'Its creators allowed it to move matter, time and dimensions, create machines, and compute the Universe. Unfortunately, after the problems Dax and Reniola caused by taking mortal forms, they decided

149

not to allow an entity that powerful to do the same. Are you going to change your mind about our agreement now you have control of your mind back?'

'My mind couldn't be any more changed after what Tacal Tehalt did to it.'

'Do you want your own body back?'

Kulp had no choice. Even the alternative of spending eternity with Tacal Tehalt, tweaking switches against his better judgement was no longer an option as the atmospheric pressure became intolerable.

Then it stopped.

Kulp's brain suddenly went into overdrive, but this time he had the choice to stop what he was doing despite an avalanche of misgivings. His hands worked furiously as he pulled apart and reconfigured components in the matrix control.

The Olmuke's mortal body would have been melted to a messy puddle long before he could ask, 'Does the Cosmic Corrector know what will happen if I keep crossing all these circuits?'

'Oh yes. It has calculated everything down to the last atom,' Toc assured him.

'Why am I doing it?'

'I have a prohibition against such interference installed in my programming. That is why you are doing it. Keep working.'

Kulp was too busy to argue. 'I'd still prefer to be in Diana's galaxy before this thing is triggered.'

'There will be no need.'

'Why?'

'With sufficient mass it will be possible to restore the stability the species of Dax and Reniola robbed this galaxy of.'

Kulp gasped. 'Oh no - This wasn't your idea was it?'

'Diana's.'

Kulp's android fingers struggled to keep up with his brain. 'Yes, I suppose it was.'

CHAPTER 63

Salisbury was surprised to that find his car was where he had parked it when the dinosaur nightmare started. It was probably the reason he hadn't been returned to his home with its misty, rolling fells. It would have helped if his memory of events had been wiped clean. As virtually everyone else on the planet would not be able to remember their scales, vegetarian diet and the tyrannical Dozaurs, it didn't seem fair.

Salisbury couldn't go back home until he had made sure the others had returned safely. He turned the key in the ignition, expecting it to have seized up after spending so long on the flood plain of a wide stream. But there wasn't so much as a beaver's footprint on the bonnet and the engine started up right away.

When he reached Diana's terraced cottage Julia and her cousin, Zoë, were being very enigmatic about where she was, so Salisbury didn't press the point and drove up to the observatory. It may have been his imagination, but birdsong wasn't at full throttle given the time of year, and a couple of hares were trying to outstare each other instead of boxing themselves to a standstill. Perhaps they could remember what had happened. After being persuaded that they were lizards, they were probably trying to remember how to go about things.

Eva was back to her usual self, busy bullying Fiona about the observatory. She obviously hadn't been intimidated by a universal reality that had more to do with a Tinkerbell dimension than astrophysics. So Salisbury left the astronomers to set the heavens to rights and strolled across the meadow to Yuri's cottage.

He was sitting on the roof.

'What are you doing up there, old man?'

'The wall, it is gone, and Trotter woman wears jodhpurs too tight to climb drainpipes.'

'I thought you were convinced she was an illusion?'

'Julia says Trotter woman wants to see me. If Julia can pass on message from her, she is not illusion.'

'Don't take on so. It's not as if she remembers that she was going to kill you.' Salisbury indicated the sky and meadow and threw his arms wide in the bracing air. 'Look, everything is back to normal. None of us were behaving rationally in the other place.'

'What other place?' interrupted a sharp voice.

Salisbury spun round and thought fast. 'Day trip with some students. Things became a little surreal. Still can't handle their lager.'

'Oh.' Daphne Trotter was hardly surprised that he allowed adolescents to drink.

'You wanted to see Yuri?'

'Yes. When is he coming down from the roof?'

'Probably when it rains heavily enough. Can I give him a message?'

Daphne thought carefully, was about to speak, then changed her mind.

'You can trust me, and it would be better than shouting it,' Salisbury persuaded her.

'All right.' At the risk of sounding absurd, because she had no idea why it bothered her, she asked, 'Does he have a cat?'

Salisbury blinked. 'A cat?'

'Yes. Leg at each corner, long hair and bad attitude - one rumour even claims it can talk.'

'I don't think so. Why?'

'Edna is being bothered by this large cat. It scared the cows in the lower meadow not so long ago. Must be his.'

'I'll ask him.' Salisbury was about to call up when Daphne opened her Burberry raincoat and pulled out an airgun. 'Only I don't want to have to shoot it, at least not without telling its owner first.'

As soon as Yuri saw the airgun he vaulted the ridge tiles and rolled down the other side of the roof.

'What is the matter with that man?'

There was a yell as the astronomer crashed into the nettles in the back garden.

'Must think you're going to shoot him.'

'Shoot him - Good grief! I wouldn't waste the shot.' She gave up and strode back to her Land Rover.

Salisbury went round the back of the cottage to pull Yuri from the nettles.

'You should really do something about this garden.'

'Why? Would pansies have broken fall?'

'You need a bit of gardening to keep you occupied, and then you wouldn't feel the need to climb onto the roof.' Salisbury kicked aside an old zinc bucket which Yuri had fortunately just missed. 'For goodness sake pull yourself together. You've got to get used to the idea that it's all over.'

'Perhaps I like being paranoid.'

Salisbury helped Yuri limp inside.

'Daphne Trotter only wanted to know if you owned a cat?'

Yuri scratched his head. 'Cat? She knows I do not own cat. Why?'

'She's going to shoot it.'

'That is her remedy for everything.' Yuri threw himself onto the sofa. 'I think I shall now die.'

'All right, I'll make a cup of tea while you're doing it.' Salisbury went into the kitchen and called back, 'Has Diana returned yet.'

'Where did she go?'

'Julia isn't saying. I don't think she knows.'

'It is like Diana to be in thick of things when aliens are around.'

Salisbury switched the kettle on and brought in a tray. 'I'm rather glad she wasn't. I don't like the idea of her being chased by dinosaurs or battling android armies with that obnoxious Olmuke creature.'

'But she does this so well, and someone must do it...

She will come back as soon as she has saved Universe.'

'No doubt with the help of a couple of Olmuke.'

'This is very likely.'

CHAPTER 64

Tacal Tehalt returned unexpectedly and realised that Kulp had been reconfiguring the portal instead of being dead.

The Olmuke and that android should have been crushed. Instead, both of them had broken free of the matrix computer's control. To make matters worse, they had sealed it so nothing could get in to find out what they were up to.

While Kulp worked, Toc tried to talk him into escaping without his own body. The android's elegant electronic sensibilities failed to see why he would want to keep it. But the green engineer had grown attached to his obnoxious toad-like persona. The Olmuke didn't want to spend the rest of life in his sophisticated android body. Perfection was for sad losers whose sole purpose in life was invested in their appearance. He had a brain and a massive engineering intellect that had earned the right, albeit on the wrong side of any law, to be ugly. It was the badge that justified his existence, and he wasn't going to be robbed of it.

As there was no talking this Olmuke into viewing life through a rose-tinted visor, Toc would have let the Cosmic Corrector transport them out of the portal to find a ship to rendezvous with Diana and the others, but Kulp refused to move. Neither Toc nor the Cosmic Corrector could comprehend why the Olmuke was rejecting a body with such extraordinary abilities; one that could outlive his species.

Then for one lucid second, Toc became aware of what mortality could be like. To its alarm, the android realised that was all it had subconsciously aspired to after so many years of sneering at the befuddled antics of flesh, blood, bone and shell. This awareness meant that it could no longer honestly try to talk Kulp into leaving.

So Toc left him there, in the portal, staring blankly at the console he had been working on with eyes that could see infrared, ultraviolet and deep into the benighted galaxy that had spawned him. Toc felt a pang of guilt as he left the obnoxious Kulp to his fate at the fat hands of Tacal Tehalt.

The android guided the craft the Cosmic Corrector had provided through the storm of space debris being churned towards collapsar oblivion.

When he rendezvoused with Diana's ship, he was surprised at how calmly she and Gilli were taking the stormy reconfiguration of the galaxy.

Tolt and Jannu were on the verge of panic: they understood what was happening.

Diana was amazed to learn of Kulp's apparent suicide. He couldn't be serious. The Olmuke sense of self-preservation was second nature to them. Then perhaps he was no longer the original Kulp.

Diana tried to call up the Cosmic Corrector. 'Cosmo?'

No response.

'With Kulp, still busy reconfiguring the portal,' explained Toc.

'When are they going to activate it?'

'When the matrix computer is given direct access to your brainwaves.'

Diana had sometimes wondered if Julia aspired to be an orphan, but this may not have been the best way to satisfy the subconscious cravings of a hormonal adolescent.

'Nothing about this is really safe, is it?' accused Gilli Gott.

'I don't know. It's never been done before. Throwing that switch could turn all our molecules inside out for all I know.'

The wisps of the Cosmic Corrector slowly percolated out of the starship's navigation console.

'What kept you?' demanded Diana. 'I suppose you left that stupid Olmuke to join Tacal Tehalt on the journey to oblivion.'

'Yeeees... Diana. Kulp is where Kulp should be,' purred the Cosmic Corrector.

'Oh shut up! I prefer it when you don't try to talk.'

'Yeeees... Diana...'

'Well, let's just get on with it.'

Gilli Gott cast the human a reproachful glance that spoke volumes, even on her Mott features. 'What were you hoping would really happen?'

'I was hoping Cosmo would transmit me back home and send a postcard when it's all over. But I should have been so lucky.'

Sometimes annihilation seemed inevitable to Diana after she had managed to escape being killed more times than was natural for a lucky cat.

'Okay then.' She turned to the others. 'Been nice knowing you - mostly. Let's give this galaxy a makeover.'

Tolt and Jannu obviously didn't believe she would dare do it until she ordered the Cosmic Corrector, 'Take me to that crazy Kulp and hope that Tacal Tehalt hasn't had time to think up something too creative to do with him.'

CHAPTER 65

When Kulp came round, his pounding headache shouldn't have been possible in the circuits of an android body. He twitched suddenly and felt corporeal reflexes. Being

156

so determined to return to his own body perhaps hadn't been such a good idea after all, especially when it was the doing of Tacal Tehalt.

The Olmuke didn't want to think about why the Kleet had done it. At least there had been no deterioration in the green body, but his brain was having trouble adapting. He now missed the speed and acuity of android circuits. With them he could have carved out an empire for himself, assuming the Kleet controlling him fell into a black hole.

Tacal Tehalt hadn't been able to understand why he had lost control of Kulp's mind. He sent the malfunctioning android body away to be checked over while returning the Olmuke to his original body and confining him to a cell where he could reconsider the benefits of a life without pain.

Kulp cursed himself for gambling that Diana and the Cosmic Corrector would be bothered about what happened to him. He should have realised that an entity powerful enough to turn his galaxy inside out wasn't going to bother about one of its criminals.

Absorbed in his own private dungeon of discomfort and resentment, Kulp didn't immediately notice the figure pressed against a wall to avoid the scanners. He was so surprised he almost called out.

'Shut-up!' hissed Diana.

She dropped onto all fours to scramble over and key in the code that released his shackles.

The Olmuke was too stiff to move right away. 'What are you doing here? Do you want to get killed as well?'

'No, I've just discovered a more exciting way of ending it all.'

'What?'

Diana looked intently at a far corner. 'Cosmo.'

'Yeeees... Diana...'

'Stop saying that! It's really annoying!'

Before Kulp could remember where his knees were,

157

both of them were suddenly inside the satellite's control portal.

Diana put on the matrix headpiece.

Kulp realised what she was doing. 'No! You'll be killed!'

But the matrix recognised her brainwave pattern before the feeling returned to Kulp's body and he could stop her.

For a moment nothing happened.

'Do you know what you've done?' the Olmuke protested.

Diana smiled. 'Oh yes.'

'You cannot survive in a positron Universe!'

'But this galaxy can. It's where it came from. Ask Dax and Reniola about it when you meet them on the other side.'

There was no noise.

A rippling white light welled up from the satellite's core. In a billionth of a second it spilt out of Tacal Tehalt's space station and engulfed the galaxy accreting about its new black hole. That corner of space being sucked into oblivion suddenly went out like a light.

Simultaneously another galaxy lit up.

It was trillions of times more vibrant.

Kulp looked down at his body.

He was no longer as grotesque as he deserved to be and gleamed with a silver-white aura.

The levitation cushion fell from beneath Tacal Tehalt. The tyrant rolled across the floor, reduced to the huge, cracked, semi-intelligent egg he had hatched from.

Gilli was amazed and delighted to discover that she had the ability to change shape. Toc's artificial body was now pliable and warm, and swamped by the aromas, sounds and wavelengths it had only experienced through electronic sensors.

Tolt and Jannu remained more or less the same.

158

Outside the ship the reborn galaxy gleamed, its sky ablaze with stars and, beyond it, other galaxies.

There wasn't so much as a red giant or hydrogen cloud to be seen.

CHAPTER 66

'Have you ever considered that there is a reason for not seeing things as they really are? And that enlightenment can only evolve through mortality? Busy, busy mortality, occupied, stressed, engaged in altruistic acts - or perhaps murder - but always building, destroying and rebuilding. Without being limited to those tangible three dimensions, what is the point in immortality without creativity? To build castles of cosmic cobwebs with pure thought? Weave star systems with profound awareness?

'Or, because I am questioning the immortality conferred on me, does that mean I never really belonged to your dimension? Given the way our species ascended we were never entitled to be here in the first place. So let's all get in the queue, behind Kulp and his cronies and clamber back up that greasy pole. Then - eventually - we might find the enlightenment we really deserve.'

There was malicious satisfaction in the way Dax expressed her contempt for the Superior entities she had once believed infallible.

'You gave the Cosmic Corrector the power to choose someone with an imagination to rectify the damage our ancestors caused in their drive for immortality. Meet mortality's revenge. As we evolved at the expense of the galaxy that spawned us, this is payback time. Just be grateful nothing worse happened; we all deserved it. The Cosmic Corrector, despite all the restrictions you imposed, knew what to do and found the right person to allow it. Now, in this dimension, everyone is enlightened, even Kulp and his friends. It serves you puffs of pomposity right.'

The Supreme Guardian could not believe she was being faced down by the very individual blamed for causing the planet dweller catastrophe.

Was it was time for her enlightened species to accept the blame and start again at the bottom of evolution's ladder?

Dax was right. They had been the ones to destabilise the galaxy's black hole, committing it to slow decline deep in a fold of space-time where it had been doomed to prematurely peter out.

'All right,' accepted the Supreme Guardian. 'We must recall the Cosmic Corrector while we still can. It cannot be let loose to follow its own devices.'

'That's too late. It now has a mind of its own.'

'It's too dangerous when operated by a mere mortal. You and Reniola must find it. By the way - where is Reniola?'

CHAPTER 67

Fiona flopped down onto the chair before the spectrographic display screen. 'That's funny. I suddenly feel quite odd.'

Eva didn't bother to look up from her keyboard. 'Not surprised after the different atmospheres we've had to breathe.'

'It felt as though a hole had suddenly been punched through space.'

Eva looked up, quite prepared to believe the worst. 'Whose space?'

'I'm not sure, I could swear that something has been violently wrenched away.'

Eva shuddered. 'Now you come to mention it, Yuri swore blind that another galaxy was linked to ours by a gravitational anomaly.'

'It would tie in with what that alien told us.'

'You mean, our Universe is like crumpled paper, with wormholes created where the folds touch each other?' Eva grimaced at the unscientific analogy, wondering how it had managed to escape her mouth.

'In more than four dimensions of course.'

'That's one theory you're welcome to work on without any interference from me.'

Despite Eva's voice being loaded with sarcasm, Fiona now had the bottle to stand up to her bullying boss. 'But I like it. The premise works for me.'

'I like apple Danish, but white sugar brings me out in a rash.'

'You also like playing with shotguns, and it's pure luck you haven't killed anyone.'

'Okay, so go ahead and write up your wonderful theory to join all the others floating around out there. The tricky part will be proving it - as well you know.'

'But if it's true ...'

Eva cast Fiona a pitying look. 'Truth has nothing to do with it. Revelations only come out when the human mind is ready for them. You're better off with the Big Bang until fashion says otherwise... unless you want to revisit Fred Hoyle.'

'You're not very adventurous?'

'So why do you think they let me run this place.'

CHAPTER 68

After watching hours of documentaries about eco-disasters and pollution in general, Julia was satisfied that the world was back to normal. It was once again the place where her resourceful cousin, Zoë could sally forth and do green combat with the forces of greed, road builders, fracking companies and the manufacturers of gas guzzlers.

The teenager and young woman packed their knapsacks with lunch, posters and spray cans, and left to find dog poo to stick flags in and suitable fly posting spots out of CCTV range - on Daphne Trotter's land you could never be sure who was watching you.

The occasional rabbit bobbed up to regard them with a mixture of suspicion and disbelief as though wondering who was on the wrong planet, although the din the jackdaws were making suggested they knew they were descended from dinosaurs and had every right to be there.

The report of a shotgun in the far distance meant that the gamekeeper, Bert Wheeler, was experiencing no conflict about his true identity. Whatever else was wrong with Daphne Trotter, her land was surprisingly eco-friendly to ensure that her and her friends would always have something to shoot.

As Julia and Zoë passed Yuri's cottage on the way to the museum, the teenager decided not to call in when she saw Salisbury's car parked nearby. She was also tired of having her grammar corrected. With a brain wired to speak correct English it would only destroy her enjoyment of those slices of pseudo realism, the ubiquitous soap operas. Salisbury was a man who had never composed a text to anyone.

Managing to persuade Zoë that the large, hairy creature thudding through the long grass was a local badger which would turn very nasty if disturbed, they strolled into the museum grounds to look at the radio dishes.

Yuri observed them over the rim of his cup as he sat in his back garden sipping tea. 'Mrs Eva will not like them wandering near those.'

Salisbury was getting used to Yuri's flights of fancy interspersed with the occasional profound statement. 'Zoë and Julia are hardly going to cause vibrations strong enough to affect a radio telescope.'

'I think Julia, she should be astronomer.'

Salisbury shook his head. 'Doubt that she could spell it.'

'One day she will be old enough to watch sky instead of soaps.'

'After what her mother's been through, it is unlikely she will encourage her.'

Yuri pulled himself out of the tattered deckchair Salisbury had rescued from the garden shed. 'Time to see her mother I think.'

'What makes you think Diana is back?'

'When daughter and cousin go for long walk it is either because television has broken, or mother is vacuuming up innocent dust mites. I say we go and save the last ones from carnage.'

'All right then.'

Salisbury followed Yuri down the meadow to Diana's back door. It was slightly ajar and the broken window had been glazed with an odd, mauve putty.

Sitting by the table with a mug of coffee was Diana, still wearing her camouflage gear.

Curled up on the table was a huge, angular cat.

Neither noticed the visitors.

'Well, it's your choice,' Diana was saying, 'but expect Edna to chase you with a gouge, and Daphne Trotter with a gun.'

The cat twitched its whiskers thoughtfully. 'What about a human being?'

'Oh no, please! Not if it's going to be anything like your last effort. Anyway, aren't you going to get bored after the first ten thousand years?'

'Of course not. I shall devote myself to good causes.'

'Please don't! Life is complicated enough without you trying to help out any more.'

Salisbury and Yuri looked at each other. They carefully eased away from the door and back into the meadow.

The men did not speak for some time.

'I was sure everything was over,' Salisbury eventually blurted out like one of his pupils being marked down for no apparent reason.

Yuri shrugged. 'This is optimism.'

'I don't think I can deal with the idea of Reniola roaming this planet forever.'

'Things could be much worse.'

'Yes, I suppose so. At least we're not likely to see any more of those obnoxious Olmuke, and Diana is all right. Though why do you think she was wearing those army fatigues?'

'Protest against high heels and Peter Pan collars?'

Salisbury shook his head. 'You know, I'm almost grateful for the smell of car fumes and odd spot of pollution. Makes you realise that we're home at last.'

'Ah yes, not even intergalactic super-intelligence could cure Earth of human beings.'

'Even though we certainly deserve to be taken in hand.'

'Julia's cousin and her friends, they will make protest for all of us, and then be drowned out by big business.'

Salisbury scratched his chin. 'Funny girl, that Zoë. Very intense eyes. Certainly knows what she's on about. Pity there isn't any more like her.'

'Pity she does not have some super-intelligence to help her clean up planet.'

CHAPTER 69

'Careful!' called out Julia.

Zoë sidestepped a cow pat. 'Wouldn't have thought they could wander up this far?'

'Vandals broke down the fence.' Julia sprinted on a few paces. 'Look, you can see half the county from up here.'

Zoë joined her and sat down.

'Tired?'

'Must have a blister. Difficult to get comfortable sandals made of synthetic material.'

Julia laughed, and then dashed about, knocking thistledown into the air.

Zoë mused at how everything seemed so early this year. She shielded her eyes against the sun and tried to brush away the ribbon of smoke tickling her nose.

'Don't do that,' she laughed, hoping that Julia didn't notice her talking to thin air. It was a habit that worried her humdrum cousin.

'Zoeee...' a mellow, inviting voice purred in her ear.

Zoë had never expected thin air to reply, despite the efforts she had made to save the atmosphere.

'What?'

'Would you like three wishes, Zoeee...?'

THE END

www.ingramcontent.com/pod-product-compliance
Lightning Source LLC
Chambersburg PA
CBHW070923130626
46555CB00001B/264